Eventide '96

The Tradition Deepens

by

Larry L. Hintz

This book is a work of fiction. Names, characters, places, and incidents are either the product of the author's imagination or are used fictitiously, and any resemblance to actual persons, living or dead, events, locales is entirely coincidental.

DEDICATION

This book is dedicated to the people of my hometown. To family, friends, classmates, teachers, and everyone who made up the community in which I was raised. The memories and mores that were instilled in all of us and the blessings we experienced and didn't ever realize. May we never take that for granted!

ACKNOWLEDGMENTS

Much thanks to those who have encouraged me and supported this endeavor. Special thanks to Mary Moeller who has guided me through the publishing aspect. Thanks also to my sister-in-law, Linnea Hintz, who has made sure that typos are at a minimum.

Copyright © 2024 Larry L. Hintz
All rights reserved.

THE IOWA GEM SERIES

Emerald
Diamond
Pearl
Sapphire
Agate
Onyx
Amethyst
Jasper
Beryl

EVENTIDE SERIES

Eventide
Eventide '95

Welcome to Eventide '96

It happens somewhere between October 31 and November 1. Granted that is not much time for it to take place. Maybe it happens during the night. You go to sleep in October and wake up in November and everything has changed. Your whole focus is different. Have you ever noticed that?

October can be filled with thoughts of the fall with an emphasis on Halloween. Of course there are other things going on. People rake leaves as fast as the trees shed them... hopefully. Baseball is winding down as football is just getting started, at least the interest in it. Homecoming has come and gone with all the excitement it holds.

But once Halloween is over there is a change in the atmosphere. Fall is still very much upon us and pumpkins and gourds of various varieties still abound, but the air is filled with thoughts of Thanksgiving. Plans are made for traveling to someone's house close by or far away. How big will the turkey have to be this year?

And the atmospheric aspect is also present. It doesn't always happen but when it does, it has a tremendous impact on people. Clouds display more shades of gray than you ever imagined. The temperature starts to descend as do the hours of daylight. It feels good to have the heat on.

Such is the way it is generally in the Midwest. And the people of Emerald, Iowa look forward to experiencing every moment of this season as best they can. It is the way they treat the introduction of most seasons. But something else is also present, some other feeling, some other emotion, and that is the introduction of Eventide.

Eventide is the winter festival leading up to Christmas Day. There is a mixture of the season the world sees as merely Christmas, combined with the celebration of the Christ Child.

As Eventide '96 gets closer to reality, the month of November offers a time of reflection, a time to look back at what the year hath wrought. Okay. That is not a word you hear very often. But neither is Eventide.

Reflection and Expectation

It is amazing. There are moments when it seems time stands still, and in the next second it flies by like something Tom Cruise would maneuver in Top Gun. Where did the time go? And what happened to all those feelings that went with it ... trying to catch your breath because everything was happening so fast... and it was unbelievably good? Maybe.

And now, a month later you begin to question what happened?

Was it just a dream? Or a nightmare as the case might be? You hoped that it was so you could just wake up and be done with it. But it wasn't a nightmare. It was real. And it was scary. Or it was great.

That is the way life is... everywhere. Even in Emerald where life can be kind of slow, though not too slow. And it can be relaxed but not too relaxed. Life here is simpler than in other places and people like that and don't like that at the same time. Basically though, they don't even think about it. They just live one day at a time.

At the end of 1995 two couples in particular were looking at the future and it couldn't come fast enough for either. 1996 looked like it was going to be a year of dramatic, positive changes each couple would experience on their paths to commitment, to romance.

Would the desires see fruition? Would the passion of 1995 overflow into 1996? That is what we are about to find out.

Hakeman's

Hakeman's Cards and Things has basically 3 ½ employees. By that we mean that along with owner Angela Hakeman, there are two regular employees: Shirley Nieting and Arlene Plummer. But from time to time, there are also part-time employees.

Hakeman's has become the go-to store in Emerald. And part of the reason is because of the expansion revealed leading up to Eventide '95.

And the merchandise offered is of good quality, made up of items people just can't live without. There is a good feeling in the aisles of Hakeman's. One of the reasons is because of two people working there. They are similar to one another in a variety of ways. Although a number of years apart in age, they resemble one another in appearance and attitude.

Some have even wondered if they are mother and daughter or possibly sisters. But they are just employee and employer. Angela and Arlene are the two we are talking about; each have their stories of reflection and anticipation. We start with Arlene.

Christmas Day 1995

He was all smiles Christmas morning. The tradition for his family was to open gifts when everyone was finally up. Many families in this community had already opened gifts the night before so when they went to church on Christmas Day, kids could compare notes, find out what others got and share what they had received as well. Who got the best gifts?

Opening gifts on Christmas morning was part of this family's tradition and that tradition also carried through in not going to church Christmas Day. It was about half and half in Emerald households.

Now it seems the younger you are, the more excited you get opening presents. That is not to say you don't appreciate them. You still do. But other things take priority. In the Seagren house the usually spotless living room carpet is covered with bits of discarded wrapping paper, bows, and ribbon. The decorative paper once held secrets but now all secrets have been revealed. And smiling faces revealed a feeling of joy to all in the room.

One face was smiling but it was not because of any gifts received, but for another reason. No gift could match the feelings he had this sunny morning. Brian looked around the room and tried to join in all the excitement, but his one thought, the one thing on his mind, was Arlene Plummer, the one with whom he was in love. He hoped he would talk to her sometime today.

This romance started during their senior year. They were together and seen as a couple even though Arlene was still pursued by another classmate. When the next school year started and Brian and Arlene were moving in two different directions, they made the decision to ... just see how things went, a decision neither really liked, but was made, nonetheless.

Well, how did that decision turn out? When they got back together around Thanksgiving, it was evident that neither wanted to be with anyone else. The passion shared ignited between the two like they had never experienced before.

And now, on Christmas Day, Brian has that nagging desire to be with Arlene. And truth be known, she wants to hear from him as well. What will become of these agonizing desires?

Arlene's Christmas

Just blocks away sits a young lady dressed and waiting to head to church. She is wearing Christmas gifts from her boyfriend. Around her neck is a beautiful red necklace, her birthstone. Her ears feature pierced earrings to match. She hopes people notice her new jewelry and she can tell them that it all came from her boyfriend, Brian.

Her family opened gifts the night before and she was happy and thankful for all she received. On the other hand she really couldn't have cared less if she received anything. Sitting on her bed she has all of Brian's love letters scattered on her spread. From the very first one to the last, she has reread them all.

She looks to her dresser where Brian's framed graduation picture finds a place of prominence. She wonders if her Christmas wish of talking to him today will come true. It is hard for her to think of anything or anyone else. Yeah, she too, has it bad.

She hears from the other side of her bedroom door, "Arlene, you ready to go? It's almost time."

"Be right there, Mom." She gathers the letters, stacks them neatly and deposits them in the drawer right beneath Brian's picture. She puts her coat on and joins her parents as they head out to the car.

A light coating of snow was delivered overnight, nothing to be concerned about. God's gift for this special day. Tire tracks reveal not a whole lot of people have been out this morning. As they neared St. Paul's Lutheran, the number of cars doesn't come close to matching the number the night before. Typical. Still, it felt festive as they entered the brick building.

Looking around she saw people she knew. But there was one special surprise. There, sitting about halfway up on the right side sat a person she didn't expect to see. Much to her surprise she saw her best friend, Brenda Cooper, sitting with her boyfriend, Jared Emerald. Huh! That was a first. But now she would have someone special with whom to talk after the service. Someone with whom to share a lot of juicy details... or not.

After The Service

As the congregation is ushered out, Brenda saw Arlene sitting on the other side. She gave a huge smile and a not-so-subtle wave as she walked out of the sanctuary. Jared also smiled but didn't contribute the same sentimentality.

As Arlene made her way out, Brenda was waiting for her. Arlene was the first to say something. "What are you doing here?"

Brenda and her family were members of Grace Methodist

although rarely attended. They did go the night before on Christmas Eve. "Well, my family wasn't going to church this morning and Jared asked me if I wanted to go and then come over for Christmas dinner. My family was all sleeping in and, I don't know, I decided to come today."

"Good for you." And they talked a little before getting their coats on. Once again, it wasn't very crowded. "Get anything special for Christmas?"

Brenda said, "You mean a ring?" She gave a look that said, fat chance. "No. How about you? I mean besides what Brian already gave you."

Arlene raised her eyebrows and said, "Well," giving the impression she got something special.

"No," Brenda said thinking that Brian had proposed. She took Arlene's now gloved hand and said, "is there a ring in there?"

Arlene smiled, "Well, no there isn't." And then she continued by lifting her chin indicating her necklace. "But there is this."

"Oh, you showed that to me already." Brenda looked at the necklace Brian gave Arlene. "I will have to say, that is beautiful."

Then Arlene turned her head to show off her earrings.

"And matching earrings as well? They are so pretty." Then Brenda pulled Jared over and said, "Hey sweetie," with a smile on her face. "Look what Arlene got from Brian."

Jared looked at the jewelry. "Pretty nice."

Brenda made sure Jared saw the gifts and Jared knew he better step it up a notch in his gift giving in the future. A lot of kidding around.

Another Couple

And last but not least, on this Christmas morning, 1995, another couple is enjoying this festive day. Angela Hakeman and Noel Dahlke, as of late, have become a very serious couple. A turning point with these two has taken place over the last month.

In the last year their relationship was up and down basically because Noel had trouble figuring out just what he wanted out of life. An entrepreneur known for a mind that went a hundred miles an hour in various directions, was on his way to slowing down and settling in a place where a meaningful relationship could find a foundation.

As of this last year he moved his headquarters from Mason City to Emerald, and not in a shy way. His business took up a big portion of a small strip mall on the highway. And he had helped Angela expand her business, a huge success as Eventide descended on this community. It was so successful that even before the end of Eventide, other business were seeking his counsel and advice.

These two were very close to the next step in their relationship: marriage. And on this Christmas Day they seemed to be practicing what that would look like as they spent the day together. Everything was going great from the meal they prepared to the ambiance of her place, to the wine before dinner, and the general feeling of spending the day with the one you love.

But then the unexpected phone call came and that changed everything. Angela got a phone call from her brother. Leading up to Christmas as they were putting up the tree, Noel found pictures of Angela with this older guy and suspected a romantic relationship of the past. However there was no romance involved. Angela explained that it was her older brother and that they weren't very close. In fact she didn't even know where he lived or the last time they had seen each other. Maybe it was at their grandmother's funeral. And now she gets a phone call?

"Glenn? Is that you?"

"Yeah, Angela. It's me. Kind of a Christmas surprise, huh?"

"I guess you might say that." Angela responded. And then there was a quiet time for a few seconds.

Noel could tell he wasn't talking, and Angela wasn't talking. There was just silence between the two.

And then Noel was surprised with what Angela said next because it didn't sound like the Angela he knew.

"What do you want?"

Noel thought that was a strange way to talk to her brother. "I guess they aren't very close," he thought.

But after the question, there was silence again. This was really strange.

Glenn answered, "I guess I deserve that."

Angela didn't respond, just waited for him to go on.

"Uh, Mom and Dad are here with me."

"Where is here?"

"Joplin, Missouri."

"Okay. What do you want?"

Silence for a moment and then Glenn said, "Uh, Mom's not doing so good."

"Mom?" she thought. Dad is the one who was sick. Angela asked, "What's wrong? What happened?"

"Well, they think she had a heart attack. She's in the hospital."

"Oh no!"

"How is Dad?

"Not so good either although he is not in the hospital. He is here with me."

"Can I talk to him?"

"No. He is sleeping right now. The doctor gave him something. He was really upset."

Angela looked over at Noel. "Noel, would you mind? I need to talk to my brother for a little bit. I am going to take this in the bedroom."

"No problem. No problem." Noel had a blank look on his face.

Angela closed the door behind her. All Noel heard was a muffled conversation for the next few minutes.

Any Explanation?

Noel didn't know what to do with himself. He did some cleaning in the kitchen and then went into the living room and turned on the television. At times he could hear Angela getting kind of loud and then there were hushed comments. The conversation went on for about ten minutes and then there was silence. When Angela came out of the room he could tell she had been crying.

Noel got up right away and went over to give her a hug. "Everything alright?"

She leaned onto his shoulder as he wrapped his arms around her. She cried a little bit and then put a tissue to her eyes. She gave a huge sigh before saying, "Let's sit down." And before she went on she asked, "Would you get me a glass of wine?"

He jumped up. "Sure. Sure." He went into the kitchen and got them both a glass of Cab. This was hardly a romantic time, but what Angela wanted, Angela got.

She took a sip and then just sat there for a moment.

"Are your parents okay? What happened?" Noel was curious.

She told him basically what he had already surmised from what he heard of the conversation. And then she went on to explain a little further. "Mom seems to be okay. But with whatever Dad had before they left, well, it all gets complicated."

"So they are at your brother's house in Joplin?"

"I guess they made it that far and were going to stop in and see him..."

"So your parents knew where he lived?"

"I guess. Anyway, it was while they were there that Mom felt funny and... bottom line they took her to the hospital. Supposedly she is doing fine."

Noel had more questions but didn't know if this was the time to ask them or not. He treaded softly. "So, are you going to call later and find out more?"

She looked at him. "I guess."

"What is it with you and your brother?"

Angela looked down and rubbed her forehead. "Oh Noel. I guess I will have to tell you sometime about the whole situation. But not now. Okay?"

"Sure. Sure. Whenever you are ready. But know that I am here to help in any way I can. Okay?"

She reached over and squeezed his arm. "I know. I know. And I, I am so thankful you are here. And I will explain everything... everything soon. It is just a lot to take in right now."

"I understand." Although he didn't but that was part of being with Angela, just being there.

The rest of the evening was kind of weird. But the awkward aspect did finally dissipate as they sat together on the couch. They both appreciated the presence of each other. That would help in the future.

New Year's Eve Plans

New Year's Eve was on a Sunday this year and it was the beginning of the last two weeks of Christmas vacation for Brian. He and Arlene wanted to make the most of these two weeks before he had to go back to Iowa City. The last week of 1995 they were together as much as possible. But they also enjoyed being with Brenda and Jared. It was while they were together at Pop's Pizza that the question came up.

"What are we going to do for New Year's Eve?" Jared asked the question with the assumption that they were all going to be together that night. And that got everyone thinking about spending at least part of the night together.

"Well," Brian said looking at Arlene. "We could, uh... go out to eat. You know, maybe The Dock?" He looked around to see what kind of response he might get. Nothing.

"Or we could go to a movie together."

"Yeah. That could be fun."

"What do you think, Arlene?"

Arlene played with her bottom lip for a while and then said, "Well." Everyone waited for her to continue. "I like the idea of maybe getting dressed up and going somewhere to have dinner or something like that. I don't know about the movie though. Maybe something else?"

"Anybody we know having a party?" Brenda asked.

They all sat there and thought for a while. The only thing they eventually came up with was going out to The Dock for dinner and seeing what was happening after that. They would go out together and then see what was happening around town. Surely somebody would be doing something.

Hakeman's

"And that is all I know for right now." Angela just explained the whole situation to Shirley and Arlene concerning her parents. She didn't go into great detail about her brother.

Shirley rubbed Angela's shoulder and said, "I am sure they are going to be okay. Although this has really thrown a wrench into their plans."

"Yeah," Arlene added. "I hope everything will be okay."

Angela said, "Well, time to get to work." Traffic in Hakeman's Cards and Things was pretty light this week after Christmas. Or was it just because Eventide was kind of crazy this year? Who knows? "Time to get ready for Valentine's Day. Let's take a look at our inventory and see what we need to do next." And the three went into the back room leaving the door open to hear if anyone came in.

Angela of course had ordered new items for the store. With the added display area she would have all kinds of new items to stir imaginations and sales.

"Ange. You around?" Everyone heard Noel as he yelled. He had become a fixture of sorts around the store ever since he and Angela had gotten close.

"Back here," Angela yelled with as much volume.

As he made his way to the storage area he saw all three of them. "What are you guys, uh, gals doing?"

"What does it look like?" Angela said getting up from moving a box putting her hands on her hips. "We are getting ready for the next holiday."

"I guess you are." Noel smiled back trying to defuse any negative thoughts.

Angela smiled. "What are you doing here?"

"Just thought I would see how you were doing, any word from the folks, you know, staying on top of things."

"Everything seems the same. No news."

Noel nodded his head and said, "Well, then, I am on my way to Coopers and see if we can move ahead with their expansion."

Shirley asked, "Did they get a second barber?"

"No. Nothing like that. But they are considering another business, and I am helping them get started." And so that he wouldn't have to answer any more questions he went on to say, "See you all later." And he was off.

Pop's Pizza

Even though Arlene hadn't been a regular by any means at Pop's, it seemed that ever since Brian came home for the Christmas break, they were out there quite a bit. It wasn't always for pizza. Sometimes they would enjoy some of the appetizers offered as well.

"You know why I like coming out here with Brenda and Jared?" Brian asked.

Arlene liked being alone with Brian and so she really did wonder. "No, why?"

With raised eyebrows Brian said, “Because then we can both sit on the same side.”

“Oh, so you like that, huh?”

“Yeah, don’t you?”

“Of course I do. But I also like sitting across from you so I can just look at you.”

“Yeah, same here.” And they reached out and held hands on the tabletop until their order came.

Pizza bites, as they were called, hit the spot. Just enough but not too many. While they were munching down on them, Arlene asked, “Any more thoughts on New Year’s Eve?”

“No. Usually there is a party somewhere but haven’t heard of any yet.”

“Well, party or not, I will just be glad to be together.”

“I feel the same.”

A few minutes later some classmates entered. They were kind of loud and you could tell they had been drinking. Not of legal age yet but beer was something you could always get from... somebody. It wasn’t that hard. The group was loud but wasn’t causing problems. In that group was an old suitor of Arlene’s, Bret Nelson. Fortunately, he didn’t see Brian and Arlene and was with someone else at the time.

“Let’s go,” Arlene said. And they left.

In the car Arlene said, “I would kind of like to go to a party but ... I don't know. Don't think I want to be around a LOT of people."

Brian could tell where those comments came from. "I know what you mean. We will find something somewhere."

Cooper Barber/Stylist

"Morning Ben."

"Hey Noel, morning to you. You looking for a haircut?" Ben smiled. It was kind of a slow morning.

Noel smiled right back. "Not today. Business kind of slow?" he asked as if he was reading Ben's mind.

"Yeah, well you know. Everyone wanted to look pretty for Christmas. Probably will be slow until the first of the year." Then he asked, "What are you up to?"

"Well," Noel started, "you asked about using that extra room you have for some, what was it? Uh..."

"Scrapbooking." The voice that finished the sentence was Carolyn's, Ben's wife.

"Yeah, scrapbooking."

"You got something for us?"

Noel smiled, "I have. I have been putting together some facts and figures to give you an idea about how much it will cost to start up and what you will need to bring in to make it a paying business."

"Oh, yeah?"

"Yeah, and I've checked with some similar stores in similar areas to let you know if it has paid off."

"Sounds like you've been doing your homework."

"Well, I try to be ahead of the game."

"We will have to take a look at what you put together." Ben took the folder and handed it to Carolyn. She immediately sat down and opened it, studying the information. She noticed some suppliers from brochures that were included.

Dahlke Enterprises

Noel Dahlke was Emerald's top entrepreneur. Fred Kemp might also fit into that category. Fred started at Emerald Hydraulics after graduation from high school. He was the lowest on the totem pole. But he found his niche and ultimately worked his way up the ladder to the point where he owned the plant as well as The Dock, a restaurant on Jewel Lake.

Noel worked at Emerald Hydraulics for a while but when the

tornado of 1986 wiped out Emerald's business district, he played a gigantic role in helping Emerald get back on its feet. He didn't do it alone, of course, but he was one of the key ingredients. And the help he offered, well, it got him to thinking that maybe he had the talent to help other communities in the Midwest. And there were a lot that needed help.

Noel started his own business and based it in Mason City for a while. He was very successful. At the same time he had a love interest: Angela Hakeman. This was off and on to say the least for a number of years. He had persuaded, or was one of many who persuaded, Angela to buy into the new Emerald and open a store in the business district.

The relationship these two had was on the rocks more times than not. But as of lately, Noel moved his business to Emerald and in Angela's eyes, she was seeing a commitment to a relationship. It seemed to be moving right along those lines.

Noel had encouraged Angela to expand her store, Hakeman's Cards and Things. She did and the grand opening was the first night of Eventide 1995. It was a great success and caused other businesses in town to try something similar. Cooper Barber and Stylist was the first to seek help from Noel. But other business owners were also thinking about moving in that direction. Would what happened at Hakeman's happen elsewhere? Both Noel and the business owners were hoping so.

A New Year's Eve Thought

Jared was desperately thinking about what to do on New Year's Eve. He wanted to spend the evening with Brenda and his first thought was to go to a party of some kind. Not a big party by any means but just one where they could go together, be with friends for a while.

But no party was coming together. At least he hadn't heard of one. And the day was getting close. He thought and thought and thought. And then he came up with an idea. His parents always spent New Year's Eve with the Kemps. In fact, he could remember the first time they had it, a lot of kids were there. But that was a long time ago and now it is attended mostly by adults.

But as his parents would be gone, he wondered if he could have the house for a small party. He was thinking he and Brenda and Brian and Arlene for starters. He didn't know what they would do necessarily. He hadn't ever hosted a party, but he was thinking it might be fun.

"Hey Brenda. Got an idea. See what you think of it."

"Okay, shoot."

"Well, you know how we have been thinking about what to do on

New Year's Eve."

"You mean, crashing a party somewhere?"

"Yeah. Well I was thinking, maybe my folks wouldn't mind if we had a party at our place? I mean, they will be at the Kemp's and everything. No one will be at home." He gave an inviting stare that begged for a response.

Brenda thought about that for a while. "I don't know. You think your parents would be okay with that?" She scrunched up her face at the question.

"I don't know. Maybe." He thought out loud.

Brenda said, "I don't know. I kind of like letting someone else do all the work and just coming and going when I feel like it."

"I never thought about the work that would be involved." Jared was clueless.

"Typical guy thing," Brenda said as she rolled her eyes.

They both thought for a while. And then Brenda said, "Hey! I've got an idea. What if we had a party but it was just the four of us. You know, you and me and Brian and Arlene! What about that? We could dress up and go out to dinner somewhere and then come back, have the whole house to ourselves, play games, listen to music. I don't know, Do all kinds of things. I'll bet your parents will be okay with that."

Jared couldn't help but see how excited Brenda got. As he thought about it, the suggestion grew on him.

Brenda added. "I'll talk to Arlene and see how she feels. Okay?"

A plan was forming.

A Phone Call To Joplin

"So you are doing okay now?" Angela ended up calling since she hadn't heard anything for a while.

Joanie, Angela's Mom, said, "Yes, it was nothing. Nothing at all. I didn't have a heart attack or anything close."

"Well," Angela was going to ask more.

Joanie continued, "They gave me some pills and said I should check with my doctor down in Texas as soon as we got there. Told your father the same."

"So you guys are taking off?"

"Yeah, tomorrow morning, bright and early."

Angela thought to herself, "I've heard that before." And then she said, "Let me know how things go, would you? I mean it seems that this whole trip has been nothing but one step forward and two steps back."

"Doesn't it!" Joanie said in agreement. "We'll keep in touch. I am just glad we were here when it happened. Glenn has helped us a lot."

Angela didn't say anything. Joanie could feel the tension on the phone line and didn't say anything more about Angela's brother.

"Well, glad to hear you are doing okay. Safe travels. Love you Mom."

"Love you too, Angela."

Arlene and Brenda

"What do you think?"

"I don't know. It sounds kind of fun."

"Yeah, but you know, if there is a party, who is going to do all the work?"

"Yeah, you and me."

Arlene and Brenda are discussing the pros and cons of having a party at Jared's house. His parents haven't been asked about it yet. This is all in the planning stage right now.

Arlene added, "Yeah and I don't know how Mr. and Mrs. Emerald are going to feel about it."

"I don't know how I feel about it. I mean I like the idea of being with you and Brian and going out to eat and everything, but... I don't know... I think it would just be fun if the four of us stayed...

the four of us. What do you think?"

"I kind of agree. I like that idea. I don't want a whole lot of people around."

Brenda gave Arlene an impish look. "You probably don't want me and Jared around. You want Brian all to yourself. Don't you?" She said it in a very teasing way and raising her eyebrows up and down.

Arlene bit her bottom lip and admitted, "Well if you want me to be perfectly honest about it. Yeah, that would be my first choice." She gave a great big grin. "But then on the other hand, I love showing him off. Or should I say, showing US off. I love being seen with him. I love the fact that we are a couple." And then she got a little more serious.

Brenda saw that far-off look in Arlene's eyes. "Boy you have got it bad."

"Yeah, I know I do but I can't help it." She looked down and then asked Brenda, "Don't you feel that way about Jared?"

"Not as bad as you. I mean, I am sure we are going to get married, but we are looking at things practically, you know, getting enough money and all before we start really getting serious. You know what I mean?"

"Yeah, I guess I do. But you are always together. You work together. You see each other all the time. I, we, don't have that. I hate the fact that Brian has to go to Iowa City, and I won't see him for such a long time. I just hate it. I wish he didn't have to go."

"Does he know that?"

"Yeah, we've talked about it a lot." Then there was silence. "Hey, let's not talk about this right now or I'll get depressed."

Brenda hugged Arlene. "Agreed! Let's just focus on New Year's Eve!"

New Year's Eve—Scenario #1

"Wow! When did you get that outfit?" Jeff is looking at his bride who is wearing an outfit she bought just for the Kemp New Year's Eve party.

"What? This old thing?" Anita was happy Jeff liked what he saw: not too tight and not too loose black slacks with a deep red turtleneck sweater along with new heels that made her legs look even longer.

"Yeah, you make me have second thoughts about going anywhere tonight. Maybe we should just stay home, open a bottle of wine and..."

"Keep those thoughts in mind."

"Maybe you should save that outfit for Valentine's Day."

"Oh, I have something else planned for then."

Jeff's mind was going in places he didn't mind going. And then he got a whiff of... well he wasn't sure what it was. "And your perfume is so enchanting and inviting. Do you honestly know what you do to me?"

With sultry eyes Anita looked at him as she handed her coat over for him to hold as she put it on. He held it open and then put his arms around her and kissed her on the back of the neck. "Mrs. Emerald, you drive me crazy."

Anita just smiled, turned her head, and said, "Down boy."

As they drove over to the Kemps they noted the Christmas lights were still on in most neighborhoods. They were the first to arrive and parked to the side. A lot of cars will be around this place tonight.

They knocked on the door and walked straight on in. "Hello, hello! Are we ready to PAR-TY?"

Ginger yelled, "Anita! Now the party can begin."

A good number of people would be attending but before they arrived the Emeralds and the Kemps had a tradition of toasting to the evening, just the four of them.

Before anyone else came the two couples compared notes about what their children were doing.

"I imagine your girls had plans for tonight." Anita looked at

Ginger.

"Yes, there is a sleepover/party at the Langenwalters that all three will be at. Where is Emily going to be?"

"She is over at the Schmidt's."

"Sleepover there too?"

"Yeah. Glad they are doing that."

"And Jared?"

"Well, from what I gather, he and Brenda along with Brian and Arlene are going out to eat and then coming back to our place for a quiet evening, just the four of them."

"Did you tell them to behave?" Ginger asked.

Anita smiled and said, "I did but then again I remembered how it was at that age."

"And…"

"I pray they will." Anita smiled.

New Year's Eve—Scenario #2

She looked in the mirror to satisfy her desire to look the best she could. This was a special night as far as she was concerned. Not that she expected a surprise of any kind, but the month of December had been a rough month and with both today and tomorrow off, she wanted to thoroughly enjoy this night.

She was wearing a new dress tonight, and the accessories were also new. She felt good about her choice. Tonight there would be a late dinner and then back to her place for champagne and a night of romance ... or something like that.

Angela's phone call from her brother was still stuck in the back of her head but she was working on dismissing it completely. Her parents were probably finally on their way to complete their migration south. If she was lucky she would never have to hear Glenn's voice again. She wasn't going to let that little interruption in her life deflect from her thoughts about tonight.

On the other hand, Noel was also paying special attention to what the night would be like. He was glad 1995 was coming to an end although it hadn't been all bad. He was settled in Emerald and his relationship with Angela was going gangbusters. Business in general was looking up and he had ideas on how to improve things in a more dramatic way. And he hadn't shared that with anyone just yet. Still, the wheels were turning.

A knock on her door was immediately followed by him coming in. The evening was a little chilly and the heat felt good. "Hey sweetie. It's me." He could smell her perfume the minute he entered. It was totally Angela. And almost immediately she appeared. "Wow! You look fantastic!"

"You like it? I thought you might." She had just picked it up from Richards Clothing. It was Noel's favorite color and fit her like a glove. There was nothing suggestive about it whatsoever except for the fact that she was wearing it. It wasn't too short. It revealed no cleavage whatsoever. But it sent Noel's mind in a direction he didn't need to be shoved into.

He hadn't purchased a ring yet, but tonight was going to seal the deal for both of them that when Valentine's Day came around they would be announcing to the world (Emerald) that they were soon to be married.

"Ange, you are beautiful." And he leaned in to give her a slow kiss, which she returned. They stood there in a warm embrace and then... the phone rang.

New Year's Eve—Scenario #3

He had been looking forward to this night even though it marked another day closer to having to make that long trek back to Iowa City, that long drive in the opposite direction of where he wanted to be, that long drive away from Arlene. Still, he was looking forward to tonight. He would be celebrating New Year's Eve with Arlene. It was no ordinary night. They would go out to eat with Jared and Brenda. They would come back to Emerald and spend the rest of the evening at Jared's house at least until probably one in the morning or something like that. Being with Arlene the whole time was almost more than he could grasp. And what will make it even more exciting is that she will be wearing the dress she wore to the Christmas Dance.

She actually didn't want to wear it as she had just worn it to the dance not all that long ago. But it was a special request by Brian. And in a way, she really liked the dress and since he thought she looked great in it, why not? Anything for her guy!

They all met at Jared's. His parents had just left for the Kemps and so it was perfect timing. Arlene and Brenda put together snacks for later and deposited them in the refrigerator. Then they were off. Jared was driving and so Brian and Arlene were in the back seat. No problem whatsoever.

"Okay, you two," Jared looked in the rearview mirror and seeing them sitting close, Brian's arm around Arlene, he said "I will be keeping my eye on you guys. You better behave."

"You just keep your eyes on the road," Brian said. "And both hands on the wheel."

"Well that is not going to happen," he pulled Brenda closer.

And when Jared was looking, Brian pulled Arlene close and gave her a kiss that lasted longer than Jared thought it should. "Next time you drive Seagren."

They wanted to get reservations at The Carriage House but were about two weeks late in calling. It filled up fast. Their second choice was Cardigans and they had to move the time around a little but were able to get in.

In spite of the fact that the trip started with a passionate kiss being exchanged both in the front and the back, the conversation for the trip was pretty lively both on the way there and the way back. These two couples were having a lot of fun.

At this time the evening traffic wasn't too bad. In a way they were glad they had the time they did. Later driving might be a little more challenging and you never knew who would be out or how much alcohol was in their system. No problem at this hour. At least that is what they thought.

When they finally got back to Jared's the guys hung up all the coats while the girls got all the snacks out and ready for later. They watched their babes working together as they sashayed around in their beautiful apparel. Both were thinking of what it might be like later in life when they would all be married.

The night was going very well. They played some board games. They even found themselves sitting on the floor for a while. Girls kicked off their heels and everyone got comfortable. The television was on, and it was getting close to the time the ball would come down in New York. They didn't have any alcohol and they didn't need any. Right now they were practicing for later as each couple was taking their time necking as if no one else was around. The lights were low. Candles were burning. Perfect ambience.

Then they heard the back door open. Footsteps coming up the stairs. Whispering was muffled. Someone was coming in.

"Anybody home?"

No one moved. They were all sitting on the floor. Were his parents' home already? The light was turned on in the dining room which brightened up the living room a little.

"Uh, Happy New Year... everybody."

Everyone recognized the voice. In walked Jake and Rachael.

"Jake! What are you doing here?"

Everyone was surprised. But the person everyone was wondering about was Arlene. Even though she had come to terms with Rachael and Jake, no one, not even Arlene, knew how she felt about being at the same party with her and Arlene's old boyfriend, Jake.

Jake said, "Didn't know you guys would be here." Then he smiled. "Do Mom and Dad know you are here?"

Jared said, "Yes. Mom and Dad know we are here. They said it was okay." Everyone got up off the floor and the living room lights were turned on. While it was a little awkward at first, it gradually got more comfortable.

One of the things that made it more comfortable was when Rachael made the move to start talking with Brenda and Arlene. Before long the three of them were talking away leaving the guys wanting to get back to what was going on before being so rudely interrupted.

The night ended with some champagne Jake brought up from the basement. He knew his dad had some down there for special occasions. Arlene had never had champagne before. She enjoyed it but it made her a little dizzy. The little amount she had also made her feel a little less inhibited. Her first taste of alcohol. She would remember the night.

The Phone Call

It got to the point that whenever the phone rang, she got nervous. Ever since her brother called to tell her about their parents, she was a little leery. She had a problem with her brother from years ago. Their relationship was not a good one and for good reason. She didn't even know where he lived or anything about him. And then he called with news about mom and dad.

She knew she had to take the call before she and Noel went out. She couldn't just let it go to the machine. Thinking back she could have listened to the message and gone from there. But she didn't. Fortunately, it wasn't her brother.

"Mom! How are you? Is everything okay?" She just knew that her Dad had died.

"Everything is fine. Everything is fine. No need to worry." Her Mom tried to calm her down.

"Are you down at the condo?"

"Yes, we got in last night. Nothing else happened."

"Glad to hear that," Angela said. "Whenever the phone rings I think something bad has happened. I guess Glenn calling me has started to make me feel that way."

"Why?"

"Well, he really scared me. Why didn't you tell me you were going to see him?"

"Actually we weren't going to stop. It just happened that your Dad wasn't feeling too well and then I had chest pains and we thought it might be best to stop. And Joplin was close."

"This trip hasn't been the best for you at all. Have you considered just forgetting it and going back to Minnesota?"

"No, your Dad wouldn't have any of that. We are down here now, and we've talked to our doctors so everything should be fine." And then Joanie asked, "How did your conversation go with Glenn?"

Angela took a deep breath. "How do you think it went? I have absolutely no time for him. And we didn't talk any more than we had to."

"Oh, Angela, I am sorry to hear that. Will you two ever start speaking again?"

"After what he did, I don't have any desire to talk to him. I don't think he will ever change."

Then there was a moment of silence. "Angela."

"Mom, we don't need to talk about it now. Let's just drop it. I am glad you are doing okay and that you and dad are finally in Corpus Christi. Let me know if anything else happens." And then she said, "Sorry about all this. I've got to go. Happy New Year."

She hung up and then just stood there looking at the phone.

Noel didn't know what to say or do if anything. He didn't talk for a while and then asked, "Do you still want to go out?" He suspected that maybe she wouldn't.

Angela sighed and looked at him. "That is exactly what I want to do." She smiled. "I want to go out with you tonight and forget about everything. I want to be with you. I want you to hold me and kiss me, and..."

"Hey! I get your point and I will be happy to accommodate you on anything and everything you want." He pulled her close and gave her a hard, sensual kiss.

Angela said, "Noel, I love you."

"I love you, too. Now let's go celebrate the end of this year and the beginning of the next." And they were off.

Recap of New Year's Eve

"Well, all I can say is that you are so full of surprises."

"Really?"

"Yeah. I was sure when Jake and Rachael entered the picture on New Year's Eve the fun had ended." Brenda said.

"Well, I told you before that my thoughts about her have changed a lot."

"You think?" Brenda said sarcastically.

"I mean the four of us were really going at it when they arrived. We didn't need to be disturbed."

"I agree with you on that, but I didn't mind them catching us." Arlene raised her eyebrows. "Okay, I am okay with the fact that Jake and Rachael are Jake and Rachael. No feelings for him whatsoever. But I am not disappointed that he saw Brian and me necking."

"Okay."

"And I have absolutely nothing against Rachael, but did you see what she was wearing?"

"Yeah."

"Well, who looked better?"

"You got a point."

"I guess I do," Arlene said raising her eyebrows.

Brenda squinted as she looked sideways at Arlene. "Are you sure you're okay with Rachael?"

Arlene settled down a little bit. "Yes, I am sure. It is just that... that... for the longest time I thought she was totally ... gorgeous, okay? And I felt ... felt so frumpy and unattractive. Well, I don't feel that way anymore. I know it is not a competition. But I feel attractive now. And I feel wanted and desired. Is that bad of me

Brenda?"

Brenda smiled, looked down and then at Arlene. "No. I don't think that is bad. You know, I like Rachael and she is very attractive. But the two of you can hold your own. I am glad you two are getting along. And Arlene..."

"Yeah."

"You are very attractive."

"Thank you."

"But you know what?"

"What?"

"I think you need to be careful with alcohol."

"What do you mean?"

"I mean after that one glass of champagne; you were all over Brian."

"I was?"

"Yeah."

"He didn't say anything."

Brenda smiled, "Why would he? He was having the time of his life!"

Back To School

Brian didn't have to go back to school for a week but that was not the case with Arlene. Her first and only class for this semester was bright and early on Monday, January 8. Wanting Brian to see where she went to school and wanting anyone who was interested in seeing that she had a serious boyfriend as well, to come to school with her. He wouldn't go to the introductory class, but he would be on campus. And afterwards they might go out for breakfast. At least that was the plan.

Brian drove her over and parked in a visitor space close to her classroom. This January day had all the indications that a January thaw was on the way. A light coat would suit you just fine.

They both got out of the car on his side and hand in hand she led him toward the building where her class was.

"This looks like a pretty nice campus." Piles of snow were here and there but not all that much. "More kids here than I realized. This isn't nearly as small as I thought it would be."

"I know. That is what I first thought when I came here the first day. Kind of scared me a little. But I got used to it in no time. And the classes remind me of high school a lot."

"Which building is your class in?"

"1304. Not far down."

He walked her in and took a look at the classroom. "Not a whole lot different from my classrooms. I guess if you've seen one you've seen them all. At least to a point." He looked around a little more. "Well, where should we meet?"

Arlene had a puzzled look on her face before answering the question. "Well, class probably won't be all that long, first day and all. Why don't we..." and you could see that she was thinking. "Why don't I meet you back at the car in a half-hour."

"You think it will be that soon?"

"Probably. You can walk around campus for a while if you want."

"Think I will. See you later. Breakfast, right?"

"Right."

Then he leaned over and whispered, "Love you."

She blushed and mouthed out the same words to him.

The New Assignment

Brian took off walking and saw the Bookstore, which was closed. He then headed towards the dorms where the cafeteria was also located. It was here that Jake and Rachael really got together for the first time. He didn't know that. But if he did, he would have seen the same groups of students Jake saw, not all that long ago.

Brian just did a walk through, didn't stop for anything. Time was flying by and before he knew it, he looked at his watch and knew he should get back to the car. He even picked up the pace a little so Arlene wouldn't be waiting for him. He wouldn't have needed to. Class lasted a little longer than Arlene thought. She was about 15 minutes later than she thought she would be.

He was watching the door when she came out. She looked different from every other student. First of all because she was his Babe, that was the most important reason. Second, she dressed for work which meant she didn't have on the casual garb most students wore. It made her stand out... in a good way.

"Lasted a little longer than you thought."

"Yeah, it did. Sorry you had to wait."

"Waiting for you is always worth the wait." He smiled.

"You are such a sweet talker. Let's go eat."

Perkins wasn't far down the road and the breakfast rush was over if there was one. They found a booth and placed their order.

"Well, what is this next semester going to be like?" Brian asked.

Arlene brought her folder in so she could look at it... THEY could look at it together.

"Well, I have to work with a local photographer for the next few months. But I already knew that. Just didn't know who."

"Who is it?"

"Like I said, I don't know. Let's take a look at the list and see who I am assigned to."

They went through the papers looking for her name, which should be followed by the name of a photographer.

"Here it is. Memories Forever. What is the name of the photographer? Uh, let's see." She tapped her lips for a moment. "Michael Stepchild. Hmm. That is a weird name."

"What is the address?"

"Um. Third Avenue North."

"Wonder what he is like."

"Guess I will find out on Wednesday. That is when I see him."

Brian said, "Hope he is an old guy with gray hair. Or no hair."

"Worried I am going to fall in love with someone else?"

"Well, you never know."

She leaned over the table and put a finger on his lips. "I am hopelessly in love with you."

Where was all of this leading? Neither knew. Neither cared.

Hakeman's

Shirley Nieting was busy arranging a Valentine's display featured in the new area of the store. Traffic in the store was light as everyone expected after the first of the year.

"So your folks eventually made it down to the condo?"

"Yeah," Angela said, "It was quite an adventure for them this year. Hope they don't blame it on the fact they spent Thanksgiving with me."

Shirley smiled. "I'm sure they won't. It was probably just a fluke. You get old and those things happen."

"I suppose." Angela was at that point where she put aside the whole "brother" thing. She wasn't going to let him get a hold on her. The past was the past. She got into her bookwork and deciding on what to order for the future.

The bell above the door rang and seconds later the words, "Hey Ange" were heard as Noel came into the back area.

"Morning Noel, you seem to be in a good mood."

"I am! Got some ideas to share with some of the businesses in town. Think they might like them, and they may cut down on costs and increase traffic... foot traffic, you know?"

Shirley said, "Well, that sounds kind of interesting. How do you come up with all these ideas anyway?"

Noel humbly said, "That is what I do." He said it with a smile and a wink before asking Angela if he could see her in private. Shirley went into the showroom and continued to straighten up, getting Valentine cards out and making room for more, packing Christmas cards away for later in the year.

"So what's up?" Angela looked up to him with her nose in the air and a smile on her face. Oh and she also put her arms around his neck.

"Just wanted to be alone with you for a few moments, Ange. My day wouldn't be complete without seeing you." He put his hands around her waist and pulled her close to give her a kiss. "We haven't been out for a while. What do you say? Let's go out to eat tonight."

"So you want to go out to eat, huh?"

"Yeah, but only if you want too as well."

"I guess I could get into that. Casual or dress up?"

"Your choice. And you can pick the place."

"Okay. Let me think about it." She brought her arms to the side and said, "Now get out of here, I got work to do."

One more quick peck and he was gone.

Cooper's

Walking down the street, Noel turned into Cooper Barber and Stylist. Ben was just sweeping the floor waiting for his first customer of the day. Things were kind of slow.

"Morning Ben." Noel was all smiles. "How's business?"

"Doing fine. Good to see you Noel."

Carolyn was on the other side and hearing Noel's voice came over to join in the conversation. "Hey Noel."

"Morning Carolyn."

A little chit-chat took place before Noel got down to business.

"You know, I've been giving quite a bit of thought to the proposal I gave you about expanding things, putting that Scrapbooking addition on to your store and I would like to change that proposal a little."

"You don't think it would be a good idea?"

"No. I think it is a very intriguing idea. But it also got me to thinking that maybe some other businesses might be interested in doing something similar."

"Other businesses?"

"Yeah. I would like to schedule a meeting with you and them, basically because then I would only have to ... talk about it once. You know what I mean?"

Ben shook his head. "I think so." Then he rubbed his chin. "How long before we can hear what you are proposing? We would love to get this up and going as soon as possible."

"I hear you. I hear you. Maybe next week some night. How does that sound?"

"Let's do it!"

Noel was off to find a night on which all could agree.

Arlene and Brian

"You want me to come with you tomorrow?" Brian was hoping she would say yes.

Arlene scrunched her face a little and said, "Well. I always like having you around. But I am not sure what tomorrow is going to be like." She would be meeting the photographer she would work with for the first time. "You know it could be just a meeting where we get to know each other, or he might want to get right at it. I don't know."

"Yeah, you're right. It is kind of like the first day of class. Will you get right into the subject or just read the syllabus."

They were sitting together at Pop's waiting for Jared and Brenda. Tuesday night at Pop's seemed to be the meeting point for these two couples during the time Brian was home. And even though the other couple hadn't arrived yet, Brian and Arlene were sitting on the same side of the booth.

Brian asked, "Are you nervous about it?"

"Maybe a little. But I know it will be okay. I just hope I get along with him."

"Like you do with Ms. Hakeman?"

"Oh, that would be wonderful. From the first moment I met Angela, I felt completely comfortable with her. It was great."

"Can I ask you a question?"

"Sure."

"Where do you think this is all leading? I mean, what do you want to do with what you are or will be learning? You want to keep taking pictures for... what reason?"

"Oh," Arlene was thinking about how to answer, "I don't know if I know right now. Maybe it will go nowhere. Or maybe Dad will hire me to take pictures for the paper. Or maybe I will open my own studio and take pictures like ... graduation... or engagement..." And she kind of raised her eyebrows a little looking at Brian. "I don't know."

And then Jared and Brenda walked in. And the conversation turned to other things.

Angela and Noel

They had to just get away for a while. Nothing major. It was like it was taking time to get over the holidays. Time to ... deprogram a little and get back to some kind of normal. Time to decompress? Maybe. Enough on that.

Noel and Angela decided to go to the mall in Alcoa. They weren't there to shop for anything. They were just there to get away from Emerald for one thing and walk mindlessly through the masses (not quite that big) of people there.

As they approached a Mexican restaurant they decided the aroma of what was frying was a beckoning call and they should make this place their supper destination. It wasn't all that crowded, and they found a booth that was just right for their mood tonight.

Water on the table along with complimentary chips and salsa and menus in hand they perused what was offered. They decided to drink just water tonight and get a small salad to start. Well that changed to a taco salad for both. It just sounded good.

"Well, how's it going with the Coopers? Are they getting excited about branching out into something else?"

Noel smiled because he had talked a lot about them when they first came to him for help. "Well, yes and no."

"They change their minds?"

"No, nothing like that. But I kind of did."

"Really?"

"Yeah. Ange, what you did with your place, your store, well, that was merely an extension of what you already had. You were just expanding your business, at which I would have to say, you were already a success."

"Okay." She dipped her chip into the salsa.

"And everyone looked at what you did and said, 'Wow! I want to get in on that!'"

"Yeah."

"Ange, Ben, and Carolyn are looking into going into a completely different business, one they have no experience with whatsoever. I don't think it is going to be all that easy for them to do. In fact, I think they would be getting in over their heads and have a good chance at failing."

"Well, that is kind of why they reached out to you. Wasn't it?"

"Yes. And for that reason, I think I am going to steer them in a different direction."

Angela just sat there trying to absorb all that Noel had just said. Noel went on to explain a little more until their salads came. Gradually the conversation died off as they got into their meal.

On the way back to Emerald, Angela sat close to Noel. She leaned her head on his shoulder. The meal was quite filling. Noel had his arm around her. It was quiet in the car. As he rubbed her shoulder all thoughts about business disintegrated. Those thoughts were replaced with thoughts of romance.

The Photographer

The trip to Alcoa was filled with anxiety for one thing. Arlene wondered if it was a good idea not to have Brian come along. She was a little nervous. What would it be like to work with a professional photographer? Would he be kind? Would he be nice? Would he be patient? Did she know enough about taking pictures to be at that stage of even being around a professional? Self-doubt seemed to be taking over her thoughts. At least with Brian there they could talk about it together. He could give words of encouragement.

It seemed she got to Alcoa faster than ever before which was kind of good. She didn't have as much time to worry. Parking spaces were abundant. She was early and parked a little ways from the storefront, watching to see when someone arrived.

She didn't have to wait long before a woman came, took out her key, and opened the front door. It wasn't time to open just yet. Arlene thought, "Well, maybe I can talk to the secretary, and she can make me feel more comfortable. Maybe she can tell me what he is like."

Arlene sat in the car until she saw the lights come on and then figured it was safe to get out and go into the studio. Approaching the door she saw a variety of pictures on display, evidence of the photographer's work. She barely looked at them. Still, they kind of intimidated her.

She felt the heat come on as she entered. The front desk was vacant, but she could hear someone working in the back. The secretary is probably making coffee or setting everything up for their first customers.

"Hello." Arlene was a little nervous and you could tell by the timid way she called out.

And then she heard, "I will be right out. Have a seat."

'Well, she sounded pleasant enough.' Arlene took off her coat and sat down. It wasn't long before she was joined by the woman. "Hi. My name is Arlene Plummer and I have been assigned to work with Mr. Stepchild. I am a student at the college."

She smiled and leaned on the desk. "Well, good morning, Arlene, was it?"

"Yes."

"And you've been assigned to work with Mr. Stepchild, is that what you said?"

"Yes, I have the assignment right here. I brought it along."

"I see." And with an even bigger smile she said, "Well, Mr. Stepchild is working out at the gypsum plant on the east side of town."

Arlene looked confused. "Oh no. What happened?"

She said, "Well he had to go to work." And then another smile came forth. "Let's start over. Hi, I'm Michael Stepchild. I am the one you will be working with."

"You?" Arlene looked confused.

"Yes, yes. This isn't the first time this has happened. Don't worry about it. My parents named me Michael after a well-known female actress from way back... I think." She smiled before she continued, "The only other female I know with that name is that actor who played on The Waltons. Most people that know me well call me Micky. I don't know if that is much better or not." The smile continued. "Looking forward to working with you Arlene. Why don't we go in the back and have some coffee. You drink coffee?"

"Yes." (With a lot of sweetener.)

"And you can tell me all about yourself."

And her first day began.

Arlene's Day

Seeing Arlene, or as the case might be, Brian, on an almost everyday basis, was nice but the time was coming when that would end. Still, as long as the Christmas break continued, they were going to make the most of this time together.

"So Michael turned out to be a *'she'* rather than a *'he'*?"

Arlene nodded her head. "Who would have thought. But I was kind of relieved."

"I am too." Brian added. "I don't need any competition, especially when I am going to be 5 hours away for the next 4 months or so."

"Relax," Arlene said, "As far as I'm concerned you have no competition at all." She tilted her head a little and smiled at him across the booth while at the same time stirring her Mountain Dew.

"Well, that is nice to hear." And then he went on after taking a sip of his Dr. Pepper, "So what will your schedule be like? I mean will you still be able to work at Hakeman's?"

Arlene sighed and gave a questioning look. "Well, I think so, but I really don't know for sure. I hope Angela and Shirley give me a little slack regarding my hours. I told Michael about Hakeman's, and I couldn't read her real well. I guess we will just have to wait and see."

Brian looked down and then back up. He reached over to hold Arlene's hands. "I am really going to miss you."

"Same here. It has been really nice to have you around."

And they looked into one another's eyes and said nothing for what seemed forever.

Arlene looked to the side before she asked, "Have you thought anymore about going to school in Alcoa?"

"You know, I have. I think that the next time we go over to Alcoa, I am going to stop in and get information on what they offer."

"Well, you are not going in without me. I can tell you that right now!"

Not expecting the outburst Brian asked, "Why?"

Arlene pretended to be angry. "Cause, that was where Rachael was working when Jake went to see about going to college there. And you know how that ended."

"Don't think you have anything to worry about. I would be glad to have you accompany me. I like showing off who is with me."

"I like that too."

"Hey guys, how's it going?" Brenda and Jared joined them at Pop's and once again, Arlene's day was talked about.

The Break Comes To An End

Three weeks can seem like a long time. But it gets broken up into little sections that go fast. There was the time before Christmas and then Christmas itself. And before you knew it New Year's Eve came around. And after that the time really flew by.

Brian and Arlene made the most of their short break, spending as much time together as possible. Whether it was an official date when they went out just the two of them, a meeting out at Pop's, with or without Jared and Brenda, or Brian riding with Arlene to school, they were together a lot!

But now that dreaded last night came upon them. They want to make the most of it. They dress up for this last date before Brian has to drive thousands of miles to a school far, far away and not come back for at least a decade. Granted that was a little far-fetched, but that was the way both looked at his departure.

What was tonight going to be like? How would they feel? Well, dinner was fine. The evening itself was okay but there was that elephant in the room. Both knew it was there but neither wanted to talk about it. Not yet. Not until they had to.

The car is running. The windows are fogged up. And these two are in a tight embrace. They couldn't get any closer if they wanted. Conversation was replaced with kisses that went on and on. And then Brian pulled back. He felt Arlene's tears washing his face.

"What's wrong Arlene?"

She started to shake a little. And the crying got worse. "I don't want you to leave. I don't want you to go to Iowa City. I want you to stay here with me. I want us to be together."

He pulled her close and hugged her. She continued to cry. "I don't want to leave either. I want to be with you. I want us to be together always." He kind of whispered it into her ear as he pulled her closer and rubbed her back at the same time. The crying continued for a little while but then it got less. Finally it stopped.

They released their hold on one another. Arlene took her tissue, dried her tears. Her face looked nothing like it did before. She leaned on his shoulder. "I love you so much."

"And I love you." It seemed they had said this a lot over the last 3 weeks. They weren't shy in letting this all come out. But they also felt stifled as they were in the situation they were in.

Brian said, "I don't like it any more than you do, but I have an idea."

"What is it?"

"Well, I was thinking. Maybe to make it a little easier, I thought I would come back the weekend before Valentine's Day. We could be together both Friday and Saturday. After that it isn't that long until Easter break, when we can be together and then after that, it won't be long until school is out." Hearing this Arlene thought for a moment and then said, “Well, that does sound okay... I guess. I mean realistically, we both have to continue going to school.” But then she looked up at him, “But I am still going to miss you.”

“And I am going to miss you. But it won’t be that long, and we will write like we did before Christmas.”

“Everyday?”

“Yes, every day.”

Her Brother

She couldn’t get him out of her head. The memories weren’t pleasant. She thought she had dismissed them long ago. Obviously that was not the case. And just when she thought that was a part of her life never to be reviewed again, it popped up like an unwanted dream. It was there.

What makes one sibling so different from another. They have the same parents. They have the same home. They live in the same community. And yet, one goes in a positive direction and the other, not so positive.

Such was the case with Angela and her brother a few years older. From the very beginning Glenn had been a challenge. He seemed to always be full of mischief. That was what you called it when they were young. Another term would be used as they got older, not near as vague.

Sometimes friends have an impact on you. Encouraged by those with whom you associate, you might find yourself doing things you wouldn't do otherwise. And that seemed to be the case with Glenn. Consequently things got worse.

And when that happens, parents don't know where to turn at times. Parents give a lot of leeway, thinking that maybe their troubled children are just finding themselves. And the term, "He's a good kid," comes up at various times. Usually it is said by others, giving the benefit of the doubt. But doubt, there is.

With Glenn it got worse. Stealing from his grandmother's store led to other crimes in Emerald. This was when he was in junior high. High school was a whole other story. And then he got in the wrong kind of company and drugs became a part of his life. It was downhill from there.

And just when you thought it couldn't get any worse, it did. And that was when his sister was targeted. That was the last straw. Angela didn't need to be reminded of that.

Eventide

Looking Back

It is amazing how fast things change and how important something is at one time in your life but suddenly it isn't so much at another time. We can all experience that as we travel through the days and years of our lives.

The activities you just read about, the majority of them took place in late 1995 and early 1996. These were the important thoughts that went through the minds of those starting new ventures in their lives, reflecting upon past experiences.

But all those thoughts were now part of history as NOW, 1996 nears its end. Eventide '96 is about to begin and as it does, new thoughts, ideas, ventures, and relationships all have challenges. Will anything ever stay in the realm of normal anymore? Will words once said ever hold their meaning or will there always be changes on the horizon?

This last year has been filled with opportunities, to be sure. But opportunities do not always signal something positive, not to everyone. Opportunities can mean a time for growth and expansion. But they can also signal disaster and heartbreak to others.

Angela is ready for Eventide '96. She has it all planned out. With the expansion of her showroom last year, she has all kinds of space to fill with what any shopper might be looking for. Each week she offers a new item. She really planned all year for this month of activity.

She takes time this Monday at the beginning of Thanksgiving week, to take her cup of coffee and look out her store window to see Memorial Park with all the decorations that have been put up so far. She also looks across the park to see the changes that have taken place on East Main. There have been many. And she knows who was responsible for initiating it all. Or almost all of them. Will they all be a part of the Emerald landscape permanently or will some go by the wayside. Time will tell.

But that is on the verge of negative talk and no negative thoughts are supposed to dwell very long in one's mind this time of year. Some will have to fight that, and it won't be pretty.

The Meeting

It was supposed to be just a meeting with a few businesses who wanted to do something like Hakeman's did to increase business. After all, if Angela could do what she did, why couldn't they just copy her success?

Good question but there were all kinds of reasons why her

success would not be duplicated. And Noel would present an explanation of why it wouldn't or couldn't be, along with a plan for something else for those attending this gathering.

While basically four businesses were interested in increasing sales, a good number of other businesses were also present. Eventide was Noel's suggestion back in 1990 to increase sales even in the cold of winter. And it was successful to a point. But there was a problem.

When Angela originally opened her store she only used a small portion of what was available. It worked for her... for a while. But the opportunity to expand and the need for its expansion in the community was essential for its success.

Other stores used all the space they could find, and so expansion was out of the question. And even though they had a lot to display, they really didn't need all that much room. And the cost of leasing that much space was weighing them down.

Another factor was that most of the businesses that were hurting were on East Main, basically the foot traffic was not as great as that on the other side of Memorial Park. Put all of these factors together and the problem seemed to become more complicated.

But Noel had ideas on what could be done. How he would present his solution and whether it would be accepted or not was yet to be seen. But he was going to give it his best shot.

"Glad to see so many people here," Noel began, "and kind of surprised to see so many people here at the same time. Guess word got around."

"Yeah, it did." One business owner smiled as he responded. "When it comes to new ideas or thoughts about how we can make more money, well, who isn't interested?" Light laughter came from the small crowd.

Noel smiled and looked to the side. "Well, I have some things to share, and I guess we will see what you have to say. It will be a lot to think about."

"What do you have in mind?" Stretch Odiot wanted to get this meeting moving along.

The Proposal

Noel gave Stretch a grin and continued. "For some of you... I guess it will be most of you, I think the problem might be that you have a lot of wasted space." No one made a sound, but you could tell they were thinking. "And you are paying for that space without getting the return you need. It is costing you money."

And with that statement people did some calculating in their minds. Or at least they were thinking about it.

"At the same time," Noel went on, "no one is really seeing what you have to offer since the number of people walking by... isn't that great."

"You mean we don't have as many people walking down East

Main as, say, on West Main?"

"Exactly!"

"Well, how do we fix that?"

"Good question. I have an idea." And then he looked over at the Coopers. "And I will get to your situation on West Main as well, Just give me a little time to explain."

Ben Cooper raised his hand to signal it was not a problem.

"My suggestion is that it might be a good idea to size down Douglas Hardware and Odiot's Appliances."

"Size down!"

"I know. I know. Sounds counterproductive. But realize that the cost of your lease will get cut in half as well. Half the expense. And... and it will open up a space for a new business. And that business will produce more foot traffic past your place. More exposure."

With that comment, people started to think. And that was positive. Noel had even more to share.

Eventide

Monday of Thanksgiving Week

Shirley arrived right on time. And what became a custom, or was on its way to being one, she had a container of Christmas cookies for that time when you just had to have something sweet. "Well, it looks like they are getting things set up." She looked out the window to see some city workers making sure everything was out of the way for the tree to be brought in.

Angela was sitting at her desk. "Yes, I suppose we can expect a lot of action downtown from here on out, all the way through Christmas Eve."

Shirley smiled, "I sure hope so. Are you getting anxious to set out your new merchandise?"

Angela smiled and said, "I think you are more anxious than I am. Ever since those boxes came in last month you can hardly wait to unpack everything and put it out."

"Well, you can't blame me. Those new items are beautiful."

"Yes, they are." Angela thought about the previous year. "You know, with the expansion of our showroom last year, that just seemed like a dream come true. But then again, I didn't know if it would pay off or not."

"Any doubts now?"

"No. But I don't want to get ahead of myself either."

"Well," Shirley continued, "you have to admit what happened here really brought about a change in the rest of downtown. And thanks to Noel, I think that all the businesses are going to really have a good Eventide this year."

"I hope you're right."

Eventide

Monday Afternoon

Arlene looked at what was left of Shirley's cookies. In days gone by, she might have been tempted. But she passed them up. She was watching her weight, not that she needed to. That is what most people would have said, but she had also seen those who had just let go of all discipline after high school and it wasn't pretty. She was not going to let that happen to her, no matter what.

"How come the tree isn't up yet?" Arlene was curious.

Shirley is getting her coat on, ready to go home. "Don't know. They were working on setting it up and then it was coffee break time. At least that is what it seemed. They dropped everything and all went to the café. And then..."

"Then what?"

"Well, it seemed they never got back into it after that. Don't know if something came up or not."

Arlene gave a look of "Oh, well," and got busy straightening things up and setting things out.

Angela had just returned from lunch. She and Noel decided to have lunch at Bonnie's today. "Arlene! So glad you are here. Didn't know for sure if you would make it or not, school and all."

Arlene was finishing up at Alcoa Junior College. Her focus was on photography, and she only had a semester yet to go. She had spent the first half of the year working with a studio in Alcoa where she learned a lot.

"Well, like last year, when it comes to Thanksgiving week, it usually slows down quite a bit. Same thing this year. Found out today that I won't have any more classes until next week."

"Fantastic! Hope you can spend time here. I think we will be busy."

"I plan on it!"

Arlene and Brian

When Brian and Arlene had to say good-bye and he returned to Iowa City, the departure was made a little easier by the fact that they would be writing each other constantly over the next few weeks. Brian would also be traveling back for Valentine's Day. And that wasn't that far off. And then Easter break was just a hop, skip and a jump away. And before they knew it, the semester would be over!

Add to that the fact that schoolwork needed to be done. That never came to an end, both for Arlene and Brian. For Arlene it would be a little different. She would be working with Michael the whole semester. It would be hands-on training. She would learn the tricks of the trade, so to speak.

As it turned out, she would also be able to work at Hakeman's at the same time. The training Michael provided would not be a strain on Arlene's life. She would have to be at the studio every morning, but the afternoons were hers.

She liked working with Michael. The fact that she was working with another female gave her confidence. In fact, both of the females she worked with added to her thinking along the lines she could start her own business someday if she wanted. But that thought was way in the back of her mind. Yes, she was interested in doing something with photography, but she was even more interested in doing something with Brian. She could see him as being a part of ... the rest of her life.

And then that day in late January came when Michael wasn't feeling very well. Pictures needed to be taken of a family where all the members were together just this one day. The oldest son was in the military and had to leave early the next day. It was now or never.

Arlene knew Michael wasn't feeling well the day before and wondered how this would all be handled. She had been working closely with Michael but didn't think she could handle this situation on her own. Michael didn't think she was ready either. But she had a solution.

Michael had a son, Daniel, who, at one time was interested in working with his mother. And he was quite good when it came to the business. But he was a restless kind of soul, and he intentionally went in a different direction when it came to what he did with his life. Basically, he still hadn't found his dream job and was available when his mom got sick. He could step in and take care of this dilemma.

Arlene hadn't met him yet, but he would be there to open up the shop and take care of the shoot. She was a little nervous, not knowing what to expect. She arrived early enough but found out he was already getting everything set up.

When she walked in she saw him squatting on the floor, adjusting one of the lights. "Hello." Arlene was a little timid.

He looked over his shoulder at Arlene and smiled.

Daniel

Daniel had the darkest hair she had ever seen. It was a little long, hung over his ears. As he stood up it seemed he kept getting taller and taller. He was dressed in black. A long-sleeved black shirt hung loosely on his tall frame. His black slacks revealed long legs and went down to his loafers.

"You must be Arlene."

"That I am."

"Mom told me about you. You are from the college, right?"

"Yeah, I am assigned to your mom, and she is kind of showing me... uh... the business, so to speak." She didn't really know why she was so nervous. But she was. Well, then again she did. He was very tall and very good-looking.

"Yeah. Mom said you were doing very well."

"She did?"

"Does that surprise you?"

"I don't know. It is always nice to hear that you are doing something right."

He smiled at her and then they got down to business, setting everything up.

The family arrived and in about 45 minutes the pictures were taken, and they were off. Daniel handled everything in a very professional manner as if he was the owner of the studio. Arlene was impressed at how he just stepped in and took over.

After the family left Arlene said, "I am glad you were here. You seemed to ... I don't know... do everything just like your mom would."

"Well, I have had a lot of experience. Did she tell you that at one time I was thinking of joining her in the business?"

"Kind of. But the way she talked, I kind of got the idea you were, uh... a lot younger. I don't know. Anyway, I am impressed."

"Well, thanks for the compliment." He scratched his head and said, "Uh, mom said that she postponed everyone else scheduled for today and you could leave after this was done."

"Okay. Well, nice meeting you and uh... nice working with you."

"Nice meeting you Arlene."

As Arlene walked out she felt kind of... she didn't know what. She was kind of taken by Daniel. It was not to the point of forgetting about Brian or anything like that, but he was nice. She got in her car and was about to leave when a tall, slim, woman with long blonde hair entered the studio. Was she making an appointment or... or what? Arlene would see her again.

Brian

At the same time Arlene was trying to make time fly by until Valentine's Day, Brian was doing the same thing. Oh, he would write her a letter every day. Some were longer than others, but he also delved into his studies. The more he worked, the faster time flew by.

Arriving back in Iowa City the campus looked more appealing than he thought it would. It seemed like his second home now. Covered with snow, the campus appeared to welcome activity.

He fell back into routine and for some reason, not having Arlene around seemed natural. And returning to Emerald would be extra special. Valentine's Day was not that far off.

First class was over, Brian made his way to the College Café where he seemed to spend a lot of time almost every day. The steam was rising from his coffee as he found his favorite booth. In his backpack he had his books for the next class, but he also had his stationery. You never know when that romance bug is going to bite, and you just have to write down those thoughts that won't leave you.

"Dearest Arlene," he wrote, "Even though you are not here in person, you are in my thoughts all the..."

A knock on the window moved his attention to something else. A young lady he had come to know was smiling back at him and waving. It wasn't long before she was standing next to his booth, putting her coat on the seat, and rushing to the counter for her midmorning refreshment.

This young lady was Hannah Carpenter. Brian met her last year. She worked at a store that sold much the same stuff as Hakeman's. He was looking for stationery to begin writing love letters to Arlene. Didn't find any there but it was the beginning of a ... well you wouldn't call it a relationship, but it was along those lines, with Hannah.

Hannah was from Davenport and she and her boyfriend, Kevin Ford, were attending school together. She found Brian easy to talk with and they helped one another in various ways in their individual boyfriend/girlfriend activities.

A "thank you" note from Hannah caused Arlene a little angst when she saw it drop out of Brian's coat pocket. But it also led to a deeper relationship with Brian as he explained that Hannah meant nothing to him, and that Arlene was indeed the love of HIS life.

Hannah Carpenter

She was so excited to see Brian. Christmas break was exceptional for her. Over that time she and Kevin spent a lot of time together. And it was more on Kevin's part than hers. He was the one who found all kinds of reasons to be together. It caught Hannah by surprise.

And truth be told, it kind of caught Kevin by surprise as well. He had been having mixed feelings about Hannah during the first semester. Maybe it was because he was at a new school. Maybe it was because he started to see more members of the opposite sex than he did in Davenport. Who knows why? But he got a roving eye. But over Christmas break that all changed. He began to realize how much Hannah meant to him and he wanted her to know it. And, for that matter, he wanted everyone else to know it as well.

They were together almost every day they could be. Their relationship became tighter than ever.

And when Hannah met up with Brian, she spent most of the time talking about the change that had come upon Kevin, even to the point where Brian didn't have much time at all to talk about Arlene.

Starting off the year with their occasional meeting seemed to make everything appear natural, like the Christmas break hadn't even taken place. They talked a little and it was getting close to Brian's next class when another student came to where they were sitting.

"Hey Hannah." She stood there looking at Hannah and then at Brian. A big smile covered her face.

"Oh, hi Dana!" Hannah shared the smile. "See you made it back."

"You have a good Christmas?"

"Sure did. How about you?" And meaningless conversation continued.

"Mind if I sit down?"

Hannah scooted over. And as she did Dana looked at Brian. And thinking he was Hannah's boyfriend she said, "You must be Kevin, I am Dana Albrecht.

Immediately both Hannah and Brian hurried to explain that Brian was... Brian. Hmm.

The Stepchild Family

When Arlene got to work the next morning, Michael still wasn't feeling up to par but she was there.

"Feeling any better?" Arlene gave a concerned look as she took off her coat.

Michael sniffed a little before answering. "Well, I am not at death's door like I was yesterday, but I still don't feel real well. Thought I would come in and see how long I could last." She scratched her forehead. "Hope you don't get what I got."

"I hope not, too."

Then Michael asked, "How did working with Daniel go yesterday?"

"Oh, fine, I guess. He was real nice and it seemed like he did everything the same way you do."

"Yeah, well, we worked together long enough that it doesn't surprise me. Glad he could come in and take over."

Arlene hesitated before she asked, "He said at one time the two of you were going to work together?"

"That was the plan but then, I don't know what happened but all of a sudden, he lost interest."

"What does he do now?"

Michael rolled her eyes, "Not much of anything." And with air quotes she added, "I guess he is still trying to find himself, whatever that means."

Arelene continued, "Well, he was nice to work with."

"He was kind of taken by you as well." Michael tilted her head as if to give the impression she thought he was interested in Arlene.

Arlene said, "Really?"

"Yeah, he told me he thought you were kind of cute, and… the usual stuff I guess."

Arlene was hoping Michael would be more specific, but she wasn't. And she asked, "Do you have other children other than Daniel?"

"Yeah, Daniel has a sister a little younger than him. I guess she hasn't come in while you have been here."

"What does she do?"

"She is trying to be a model or get into that business."

"Really?" Arlene didn't know any models.

"Yeah. I have some pictures of her."

When Arlene looked at the pictures, she wondered if the blonde she saw walk in the day before might have been her.

Noel's Idea

After the meeting with the businesses interested in mirroring Angela's success, and Noel's presentation of possibly sizing down, he had some explaining to do. Most business were thinking of getting bigger and broadening their horizons. What Noel proposed seemed counterproductive. And so he found himself going to each, one by one.

He started with Douglas Hardware. It was a little nippy outside but not too bad for late January. Piles of snow here and there were no longer white but had a grayer appearance. They were shrinking by the day. But before January came to an end, they would receive a fresh coating. Not much, just enough to make them look pure and white again.

Noel entered the store, took off his gloves and unbuttoned his coat as he walked over to greet Carl, leaning on the counter. There were maybe a half-dozen customers browsing the shelves. "Morning Carl. How's it going?"

Carl looked up and then gave his generous smile. "Pretty good, Noel. Pretty good."

"Glad to hear it. You got the coffee going?"

"Sure do. Come on back."

At the same time Carl said to his assistant, "Bobby, we'll be in back for a while. Give a holler if you need any help."

"No problem, Carl."

The Mr. Coffee decanter was about half-full, and Carl had already helped himself to one of the six Danishes he bought earlier. They didn't get down to business right away. Always time for chit-chat and food.

"I know what I shared was a little radical at the meeting," Noel began. "but as I explain the plan a little more, I think you will see the logic."

"I'm all ears," Carl said.

"Well, to begin with, I think you have a great business here, Carl. I've looked at your books and to be honest, I think you are doing pretty well in sales."

"Well, thanks, Noel."

"Yeah, but what might help you a little more is cutting down some of the overhead."

"Overhead? What do you mean?"

"I mean the cost of leasing the space you do is pretty steep."

"Well, yeah, but, well, I like having the room that I do and am able to spread out. It is not cramped and..."

Noel was about to interrupt but didn't want to be rude. So he just said, "I know. I know. What you have looks very impressive." He took a deep breath. "But I think it would look just as impressive, half the size, and even more efficient."

Carl rubbed his chin. "Go on."

"We can work on a new design for your store that I think your customers would like even more and cut in half the cost of your lease and insurance."

Carl thought about the money he would save. "You have ideas for how the new store would look?"

"It just so happens I do. I got these plans and pictures from a store in Carroll, and they do a pretty good business."

New Business #1

Carl looked over the material Noel brought. Dollar signs were popping up in his mind. And those signs were mixed, the cost of changing things and the income that might come in along with that which would be saved on overhead.

Noel gave Carl time to think. "I can leave this all with you. I have copies back in the office. Take your time and look it over."

Carl gave a huge sigh. "Thanks, I will."

"And I haven't even told you about one of the best parts yet."

"What's that?"

"The new business that will take up the space you are giving up between you and the library."

"You already have something in mind?"

"Sure do. Have a client who wants to move down from Fargo. He had a shop there that sold coffee, cupcakes, and ice cream. He made a pretty good go of it until a national chain came in. The competition was too much."

"Hmm."

"He has the capitol and the expertise to start up a new business called 'Coffee, Cream, and Cake.' Or something like that."

"Hmm."

"And if nothing else, it will increase foot traffic. More people walking past your store and remembering something they needed to get but have put off or forgotten about." Noel gave Carl a big smile. "What do you think?"

Carl also had a big smile.

Eventide

Hakeman's

It was that quiet time which announced itself about this time every day. Shirley had left for the day and Arlene was yet to arrive. Angela was doing some bookwork but got tired of that and needed a break.

A lot has taken place over the last year. Reflecting on all the events and activities wasn't something Angela did on a regular basis, but it seemed right at this time. Why she wasn't interested in doing anything was part of the reason. Sometimes you just get into that kind of mood. It wasn't that there was nothing to do. There was plenty to do. But right now procrastination has taken over.

All that happened between her and Noel, well it seemed like a whirlwind of activity for a while and then it all calmed down. Typical, I suppose for almost anyone's life at one time or another. And she wasn't alone. Shirley had to deal with some unexpected circumstances in 1996. And Arlene? Well Arlene had her moments to be sure. With photography, well that was part of it. But much more was the relationship with Brian. Where do you begin to talk about that?

She poured herself a cup of coffee but almost instantly regretted it. The last cup in the decanter had been the last cup in the decanter for far too long. She had to add a lot of sweetener, which she did, but one sip later she dumped it out and made a fresh pot.

Still kind of restless she walked through the aisles while Mr. Coffee did its thing. Totally immersed in one display, the bell over the door almost made her jump as a customer entered. It brought her back to reality even as she started to remember activities of the past.

Valentine's Day

The color red made its entrance early in Hakeman's as the day of love and romance approached. And customers were glad to see it. Of course there was the full assortment of cards to express everything from deep love to mild infatuation with someone of the opposite sex. But there were also little items that might be purchased to give that little boost to one's ego when received.

Bottom line, none of what Hakeman's provided could match the feelings in the hearts of two of its workers as the day approached. Both Angela and Arlene were wondering what this day would hold... if anything, from the guys with whom they were getting very close.

Arlene was just getting off her knees as she searched the drawer under one display to find the perfect box for a figurine just purchased. "Here it is. I was sure it was in there somewhere." The figurine slid into the molded form perfectly. "This should ensure it arrives undamaged."

"I hope so," the customer smiled at the perfect packaging.

Arlene rang her up and put everything into a bag with Hakeman's logo on the outside. "Have a good day!"

With the store empty she leaned in the doorway to the back room where Angela was sitting at her desk. She needed a break.

"How was your session today at the studio?" Angela asked, taking a break herself.

"About the same as always."

"You learning a lot?"

"Yeah. Yeah I am. At least I think I am." She looked off into the distance and continued. "I like working under Michael. She is so professional and seems to handle every situation perfectly."

Angela asked, "Are you getting any ideas of how you want to put your learning into, uh, practice. You know, what you might be interested in doing when you finish your schooling?"

"Well," Arlene gave an indefinite look. "I don't know. My mind goes in a lot of directions. I really don't know what I want to do. But..." And then she stopped.

Looking up at her Angela said, "It doesn't have anything to do with your boyfriend does it?" She gave a smile and waited for the answer.

Valentine's Preparation

Brian found himself once again in a jewelry store. It was the same one he was in before Christmas when looking for something for Arlene. It was where he ultimately found the necklace he gave her at Christmas. The earrings he found at another store and just by chance. He planned on only purchasing the necklace but when he saw the earrings, how could he pass them up? Now... now he was looking for a ring.

When he was mistaken for Kevin by Hannah's friend, Dana, he noticed something Dana was wearing. Dana was from Keokuk, not far from Iowa City. Her boyfriend was also from there but was not attending college. He was a little older and was working at a plant in the Keokuk area.

Dana had a ring on her finger. It wasn't an engagement ring but a Promise Ring. She had just gotten it and Hannah pointed it out.

"Is that a new ring Dana?" Hannah took her hand and examined the new piece of jewelry.

"Oh, so you noticed it." Dana smiled as Hannah turned Dana's hand this way and then another to see it sparkle. "Earl gave it to me last week. He said he didn't want to give this to me at Christmas, but also didn't want me going back to college without it." She went on to say, "It is a Promise Ring."

Brian had a weird expression on his face. "A Promise Ring? Never heard of such a thing."

Hannah rolled her eyes, "It means that Earl is saying he wants Dana to know that he is serious about her, that he will probably propose some day and that other guys should just... back off! Dana is taken!"

Dana smiled. "Well, I don't know if it means all that ... or much more for that matter. But it does mean he is serious about our relationship."

"Oh, he wants you to know he is serious all right."

And all this got Brian thinking about giving Arlene something similar for Valentine's Day and that is why he was in the jewelry store. He was looking for a ring to match the necklace and earrings Arlene got for Christmas.

Unfortunately he was at his third such store. Fortunately it did have what he wanted. And he was certain he wanted it, and she would love wearing it. Take that, Bret Nelson, and anyone else who might be interested in Arlene. HANDS OFF!

Valentine's Preparation-2

Sitting in his office at Dahlke Enterprises, Noel is daydreaming. His elbow is on the armrest of his chair, and he is half-way gnawing on a fingernail as he thinks about Angela. He is thinking about their relationship.

Noel already has reservations at The Carriage House in Alcoa for Valentine's Day. She knows they have reservations, what time and what she is going to wear. What she doesn't know is that he has already purchased the ring he wants to give her that night... at that restaurant.

They have been going back and forth in their relationship. Hot and heavy at times. At times it cooled off like an Iowa snowstorm. But now he was pretty sure that this would be the right time to pop the question. And he was so sure about her answer that he was thinking about the future: where they would live, how many children they would have, and on and on and on and on.

And then his phone rang. "Mr. Dahlke, you have a call from Carl Douglas on line 3."

"Thank you Mrs. Stillings." He pressed the 3 button. "Carl, what can I do for you?" And the Valentine thoughts did not exactly disintegrate but they were pushed to the back of his mind for the next few minutes.

A Chance Meeting

She was so focused on what was under the glass top, she hardly noticed the young lady not six feet away.

"Mrs. Emerald."

Slightly startled she responded, "Hi Arlene. Sorry, I didn't notice you ... standing almost right next to me."

"Oh, that's okay. Just didn't want you to think I was ignoring you or anything like that."

"I would never think anything like that. How are you?" And before she could answer Anita went on to say, "You are so pretty. Every time I see you I can't believe how you have... matured. You look so nice."

Arlene looked down not knowing how to receive the compliment. She was kind of embarrassed.

Anita thought maybe she had gone too far and tried to change the subject slightly. "Checking out the jewelry for something special?" And then not to appear too nosey, "I am looking for something for my husband to give me for Valentine's Day."

Arlene gave a confused look. "You are doing what?" Then she

understood and smiled. "Well, I am thinking about getting something for Brian but don't know exactly what to get."

"That's right. You're dating Brian Seagren, aren't you."

Arlene didn't know what to say for sure and so she just smiled.

Anita went on, "Brenda told me you have been going out for some time." Then she ventured to say, "Are you two getting serious?"

Now it was time for Arlene to find the right words. "Well, yes and no, I guess. I mean, he just started college and... well... we ... I guess we are..."

Anita realized she had really put Arlene on the spot. "Never mind Arlene, that's okay. I know, too many questions."

Arlene said, "No, it is not that it's..."

Anita put her hand on Arlene's shoulder and said, "I was getting too personal. Just forget it." Anita smiled. "I am so happy for you." Nothing was said for a second until Anita said as she moved on, "Hope you find something nice."

The College Café

"I thought you would be gone already."

"Well, that was kind of my plan but an unexpected quiz in my next class put a stop to those plans." Brian explained. Hannah was setting her books down in the booth she and Brian shared... occasionally. It was never planned, just happened some days.

"My car is packed, gassed up and ready to go as soon as class is over."

"You excited about tonight?" Hannah took a sip of her latte waiting for his answer, looking, and smiling at him.

"Kind of nervous to be honest with you."

"Nervous? Why? I think Arlene will love it."

"Well, I think so too but ... are we... or maybe am I rushing things. It all seems to be moving along so fast." Brian's face looked like he was really thinking. "Don't get me wrong. I want Arlene to really know how I feel and that I am serious about this relationship. But...to me this is a really big step."

Hannah gave a slight sigh before answering. "Brian, Brian. You are taking this way too seriously. Well, on the one hand you are and on the other hand... I guess you could say you're not."

"Oh, that makes a lot of sense." He was being honest and sarcastic at the same time.

"What I mean is that... that ring is not an engagement ring. It is a Promise Ring." Hannah raised her eyebrows. "I know you are serious about Arlene, and she is about you. At least by the way you have described her and ... other things. Look, if I were her and got that ring I would feel secure in knowing that we... you... you know what I mean, have a secure relationship. Does that make sense?"

Brian also gave out a sigh. "Yes. I think it does and that helps me a lot." He gave a slight grin. "Thanks for helping me see things from a woman's point of view."

Hannah bit her bottom lip before continuing. "I have a request."

"Okay."

"Could you put a bug in Kevin's ear that his girlfriend would like a Promise Ring as well?"

Brian returned a 'What are you thinking?' look.

"Just kidding." Or was she.

Hakeman's

It was going to be a short day for Arlene as she would be leaving a little early to get ready for her date with Brian. He hoped to pull into Emerald around five or so in the afternoon. She would leave about that same time to get ready. And since they would be together Saturday night as well, she was committed to working most of Saturday. She didn't mind it a bit since she would be with Brian at night.

"So, big date tonight." Angela and Shirley took turns asking Arlene about her evening plans, teasing her a little.

Arlene rolled her eyes knowing it was coming. And it continued to come.

"Do you think you are going to get something special from Brian?"

Arlene finally gave in. "I don't know. Maybe a box of candy or flowers or... I don't know. Maybe I will just get a card."

Angela asked, "What did you get him?"

"Well, since I have an ***in*** with a real photographer, I had her take my picture and I have a pretty frame for it."

"He doesn't have a picture of you?"

"He does but it is my graduation picture, and it was terrible. This one is much, MUCH better." And in kind of a snooty way she added, "I just want him to know what he is missing down there in Iowa City." She also gave a wicked grin.

And then the conversation went to the way Valentine's Day was celebrated in years gone by where in grade school you would decorate an old shoe box and you had to give everyone a Valentine whether you liked them or not.

Angela said, "I wonder if they still make that heart-shaped candy with all those silly sayings."

"You mean the sayings that made you decide who got what, like I LOVE YOU? You didn't want the wrong person to get the wrong message."

It would be a long morning for Arlene as she thought about Brian.

Finally Home

Brian was happy the weather cooperated and that the roads were cleared as he traveled west on I-80 and then north on I-35. Sometimes the trip got kind of boring but then he had his favorite radio station to keep him company. That along with the box that held the Promise Ring. Every so often he would flip it open and look at it.

Pulling into town he noticed that it was a little chillier here than it was in Iowa City. First of all, there were more piles of snow and then the sign in front of the high school that showed the time and temp every so often revealed it was a good ten degrees colder here than Iowa City. Well, it was later in the day as well.

Right now the car was nice and warm, the heater had been on the whole way. Brain got a warm feeling inside thinking that later when Arlene was with him, it might also be nice and warm.

Instead of going straight home he couldn't resist going through town. His dad always called that ***scooping the loop***. Brian had no idea what that meant but it was a saying that stuck with him. And of course, driving by Hakeman's was something that had to be done as well as driving by Arlene's place… for whatever reason.

He had just enough time to go home, take a shower and then pick up Arlene. It would be quite a night. At least that was his hope.

He thought he had enough time, but the minutes seemed to move a little faster for some reason. Looking at his watch he picked up the pace a little.

Arlene's mom opened the door and welcomed him in. "Brian, so nice to see you again. Come in where it is warm." And some necessary conversation took place until Arlene came out of her room.

She was wearing a new outfit, just for Valentine's Day. And she was wearing that necklace and earrings to match. Brian didn't know it, but Arlene always wore those treasures he gave her. Soon, she would have something else to match them.

Since it was the weekend before the holiday, getting a table at The Dock was not difficult. And that was their destination. But before they left her house while sitting in the car, they let their desires take over as a very long kiss filled them both with desire.

Eventide

Hakeman's

In some ways, this year would be similar to last year in that a lot of the new items for Eventide would not be revealed until the evening. Maybe it would become a tradition to have the new showroom partitioned off until Eventide officially began. Who knows?

Arlene is busy at work in the backroom, doing what she did last year at the same time.

"Well, how is it coming along?" Angela takes a moment to come back and see the progress.

Arlene is ready to take a break. "It is coming along but not as fast as I thought it would. Did it take this long last year?"

"I don't remember if it did or not. But Shirley was more help then than she is now."

"That's true. I hope she will be able to be back like she was last year to help, especially Friday night."

Angela asked, "Well, if she isn't, will Brian be able to help, you know, like he did last year?"

"I don't know. I can ask. He has been putting in a lot of hours at work. It would be great if he could." Arlene was looking a little sad even as she played with the ring on her finger.

She couldn't believe what happened on that first night when Brian came home for their Valentine… whatever it was. The meal was great and very romantic. But it didn't even come close to the experience when he pulled the small box out of his pocket.

She knew exactly what it was… to a point. It was a box that held a ring. But what kind of ring? When she saw the box, it took her breath away. Between her and Brenda, they had talked and joked about getting engaged but this was all too sudden.

"Uh, Arlene I have something for you." He looked into her eyes. "I hope that, um, that you will like it and wear it."

Looking at the box she asked, "What is it?"

"Open it and find out."

She was kind of shaking as she took the box. She opened it and saw the beautiful token inside, a token of ... what exactly? "Oh, it is beautiful." She took it out and put it on her ring finger. She held it out to look at it.

"It is a Promise Ring." Brian explained. "It means that I am serious about our relationship and that, if you are willing to accept it, that I see a future together." He was also shaking a little as he said it. "Um, Arlene, would you accept it?"

She bit her bottom lip and then threw her arms around his neck and said, "Yes! Yes! Of course I will." And the hug was as tight as it could be.

The Promise Ring

Saturday morning was bright and sunny, but it didn't even come close to the way Arlene felt inside. While still in bed she just stared at her ring finger. As far as she was concerned, wrapped around that finger was the largest stone she had ever seen. Although, even if it was the smallest ever, it wouldn't have made any difference. It was a Promise Ring. She was loved. And it wasn't a mere crush. No puppy love at all. It was true love. Now the question was, who did she tell first? Easy answer.

She didn't have to go to work early today. And on her way she could stop in Emerald Grocery to share the big news with Brenda. The store was busy as it was most Saturday mornings. The whole town was hopping. On a beautiful day in the winter, people take advantage of getting out.

Still a little nippy, Arlene had her winter coat on along with her gloves. Brenda had just been relieved of her duty checking people out and was headed toward the back of the store to sit down for a few minutes. When Arlene walked in, those plans changed.

"You're looking pretty nice today."

"Feeling pretty good too."

"Oh yeah," Brenda came back with. "Oh, that's right. You and Brian went out last night, didn't you?"

Arlene had a smile that went from ear to ear. "Uh, huh."

Brenda gave her a side glance. "What's up? Why the silly grin?"

Arlene shrugged her shoulders... still smiling.

Brenda knew this would take a while. "Want to find a booth in the café and talk about it?"

Arlene nodded but still said nothing.

Finally, sitting down, Arlene hadn't taken off her coat or gloves yet.

Brenda said, "You are acting so weird. You better tell me what is going on."

"Well," Arlene drew it out as long as she could. "Brian and I went out to The Dock for supper last night. Very romantic, by the way."

Brenda said, "Get to it already."

"And when we got back to town, he asked me something." Arlene intentionally stopped. "He asked me if I would accept a gift from him."

"A gift?" Brenda wondered what it could be. You usually don't ask someone if they will accept a gift.

Arlene slowly took off her gloves. Holding her hand up in front of Brenda she said, "He gave me a Promise Ring."

Brenda's jaw dropped open as she took Arlene's hand and examined the new piece of jewelry. "Wow!"

The News Spreads

Once Brenda knew the rest of Emerald would soon know as well. It was, after all, Saturday morning and customers would come in. A lot of people knew Brenda and word got around pretty quickly. Many people didn't care a whole lot one way or another. Some had her married already. Others speculated on whether or not it was one of those *have to get married* situations. Some minds always go in that direction.

When Arlene shared the news with Angela and Shirley, they too wanted to take a look at the ring. There was almost as much excitement as if it were an engagement ring. And Arlene kind of felt it was... although it wasn't. Still, it meant that a future with Brian looked very positive.

And, of course, when Anita and Ginger found out about it, a new major topic of discussion was on the table. A Monday lunch was where the news was shared.

"Well, did you hear about Arlene and Brian?" Anita was so excited about the news you would have thought she was talking about her own daughter.

Ginger replied with a concerned look. "I don't think so. Did something happen to them?"

Anita leaned forward as if this was top secret information. "Brian gave her a Promise Ring." And then she lifted her eyebrows.

"Wow! A Promise Ring?" Ginger thought for a moment. "I didn't know they were still doing that. I remember some in our class who did that. But... well... wow. I wonder if they have made plans to marry sometime."

"I don't know. I wouldn't be surprised." Anita smiled as she took a sip of coffee.

"Well, they make a cute couple."

"I know." Anita agreed. "And Arlene has really, REALLY changed over the last year. She looks like a completely different person."

"I've noticed that too. I guess, maybe more mature."

Anita shared, "Well, I think it is all because of Angela Hakeman. She has been a good role model for her."

"I think you're right." And the gabfest continued.

The Other Couple

Angela was happy for Arlene. All the excitement and the smile that never ended was translated into a very happy worker. Even when Brian had to go back to Iowa City, Arlene was still on cloud nine. It was as if she were saying, "Go wherever you need to go! I've got a ring and that says he loves me and will be true to me and… and… and I couldn't be happier."

Angela was wondering what was going to take place between her and Noel. She had a good idea that she would also be getting a ring but as of lately, Noel had been so busy with work and setting up other businesses for … something, he hadn't been bugging her as much. Still they had reservations for the evening of Valentine's Day.

She had recently visited Richards Clothing to see what they had to offer in new attire. She was looking for something new, possibly along the lines of something for this holiday. She tried to patronize local shops as much as possible and most of the time she found what she wanted. This time was no exception.

But while she was there, she also thought she wanted to get something for Noel. But what? Valentine's Day was a day that generally meant guys would get something for their gals. And they were long past the time when both genders had to give a card to the other or something like what you did in grade school.

What to get? Browsing through the men's department didn't help. She only got more frustrated and confused. What would Noel like? What would be an expression of her love? She wasn't getting an answer to these questions. She left, finding something for herself but nothing for Noel.

Of course, he wouldn't care. Men didn't seem to think along those lines. Arlene hadn't purchased anything for Brian. Maybe Angela was thinking a little too much.

The Night Arrives

Noel is just a little nervous about tonight. It is not because he is afraid he might not get the answer he expects. They have talked about the elephant in the room so many times, giving her a ring almost seems anticlimactic. Getting down on one knee is hardly the gesture he is thinking of. Then again, would Angela expect it?

She didn't seem the type.

Still, it would be during dinner that he would take out the velvet box holding an expression of his love. They ordered wine to start the night off. Most of the other couples, and it was basically couples dining out, no families in sight, had the same idea. A little wine just seemed appropriate. "Get us a bottle of your best Merlot, please."

Noel didn't necessarily like Merlot, and he wasn't sure if Angela liked it either, but he did enjoy saying the word. And that was what came out. It turned out to be not so bad. Based on the cost it should taste good, and it did.

"You look gorgeous tonight, Ange." Noel was all smiles looking at the woman he was with. It had been a long journey.

Angela looked back at him. A rather handsome and successful individual is what she saw. None of that made any difference of course. It was what was in his heart that mattered. And in hers as well! "This is wonderful Noel. I love being here with you."

"I have something special for you tonight."

Angela gives a fake surprise look responding, "Oh really."

And without a lot of fanfare he takes the box out of his pocket, holds it in one hand, scoots closer to her, looks her in the eye. As he opens the box he asks, "Angela Hakeman, would you marry me?"

The beautiful ring he has had for quite some time is sparkling as the candlelight hits it. And even though she was almost sure she would be receiving it tonight; it still took her breath away. "Oh, Noel, it is so beautiful!."

He took it out and put it on her finger.

She held her hand out to look at it and as she did, applause erupted through the dining room. They didn't know it, but they had been the attraction of the evening when one couple after another noticed the box coming out of Noel's pocket. They both were a little embarrassed as they seemed to be the center of attention.

As the applause died down, Noel said, "Thanks! But she hasn't given me an answer yet." Laughter replaced the applause.

To that she pulled him down and whispered, "Yes, I will marry you."

"Relax folks." Noel beamed with that response. "She said yes!"

Mike McCarty

Mike McCarty might be referred to as the Fred Kemp of Fargo. As Fred was an entrepreneur of sorts in Emerald, thinking of new things to do and in which to be involved, so Mike was the same in Fargo. Of course, Fargo was much bigger than Emerald. But both guys had the same frame of mind.

He started his ice cream shop in an area of town that didn't have one. It was so successful that he added something else. That being coffee and not much longer after that, cupcakes. He was doing so well that he considered expanding and franchising. Good thing he didn't.

When his success was noticed by a much larger company that could offer much more and was already nationally successful swooped in and took over the market. Mike couldn't compete no matter how loyal some of his customers were.

And Noel tried to assist him in ways to stay afloat. But it just wasn't in the cards. This wasn't one of Noel's success stories and he always felt bad for Mike.

Mike had other businesses that were more successful. In fact he came from a family that boasted of a number of siblings that shared his sense of adventure in working with the public.

Noel had Mike in mind when thinking of adding businesses to Emerald's business district. And picking up his ice cream-coffee-cupcake business and plopping it down in Emerald seemed like a good idea. Hence the midmorning call.

"Morning Mike. Noel Dahlke here. How are things going?"

"Noel, good to hear from you. You in town?" Mike had a smile on his face.

"Nah. I don't get around like I used to. I am in my office in Emerald, Iowa."

"Heard you moved, and your focus has slightly changed."

Noel was feeling good about this call. "Yeah, there were a number of factors behind the move. I am happy I did it. I guess I have refocused my ... I don't know... what I do and who I do it for.

Anyway, I got a proposition for you."

"You do? What is it?" Mike was very curious.

Noel took a deep breath and proceeded. "Well, you know that idea we had about that ice cream store you had?"

"Yeah, what about it?"

"Well, if you would be willing, I think it would be a great addition to the Emerald business district. We have just the space for it and the town could really use what you offer." Noel let it all settle in and gave Mike time to think.

The Response

Mike was thinking about the proposal. His mind was working methodically as it always did when something new came up. Whereas with some people the answer is always NO, with Mike it was more often, LET ME THINK ABOUT IT.

"How big is Emerald anyway?" And this was just the beginning of the questions Mike came up with to get a picture of what could happen.

Noel answered his questions as best he could but before he got too far he said, "Mike, if you have the time, I would like to give you a tour of the town. You can get a feel for the community and see for yourself what it might be like."

"You know, that's not a bad idea."

Noel smiled on his end. "So, are you up for a road trip?"

"Let me check what the weather is supposed to be like, and we'll make it happen."

"Sounds good. Keep me in the loop."

Noel was happy with this conversation. And Mike was happy as well.

Mike still had all the furnishings from the old store in the warehouse. He had just purchased new items with the expectation that he would be expanding. Up until now he had written it all off as a loss. But now, now things were looking up.

Eventide

Wednesday, Thanksgiving Week

Three women were just standing and looking at what they had put together. Just like last year, the expanded area would be a secret until Eventide officially began on Friday night. But unlike last year, the area was decorated and displayed in all its glory a lot earlier. Less initial things to start and an idea of how the outcome would look.

"I thought it looked fantastic last year." Arlene was nodding her head. "But compared to what we will unveil Friday night... last year doesn't even come close to competing."

Shirley chimed in. "I agree. Angela, what you ordered ... well, you sure have a knack for picking out some beautiful items."

"Thank you! And thank both of you for all your work in arranging things." Angela was pretty happy about the way it all worked out. "And I am pretty sure it will be all-hands-on-deck Friday night."

"Yeah," Shirley added, "in fact we might have to get extra help."

"I might see if any high school kids might be able to help."

"I don't think Brian can help. He will be busy," Arlene added. "But we will see."

Life had changed for all three of these women over the last year. Some of it was good. Some, not so good.

Arlene and Brian

The Promise Ring Arlene received from Brian was just as precious as an engagement ring as far as Arlene was concerned. Truth be told, Brian felt the same way. And after he left for Iowa City that February weekend the letter writing once again took off.

And while it started out the way it ended, both could tell that it wasn't as hot and heavy as it once was. They were still both committed to one another. And there was still passion involved, but at a lower level, you might say. And letters were not sent on an everyday basis. More like every other day. What happened? Life!

Many couples find themselves in such circumstances. It is not that they are any less... caring for that other person but... ultimately passion has its limits, and you now fall into a category ... a different category. And there can be a danger of taking the other person for granted. Is this making any sense?

Brian delved into his studies and Arlene found her days learning more about photography and being part of Hakeman's. Still, they both looked forward to spring break, Easter, when they could be together for a whole week.

The First Visit

Coming in from the north the first sign he saw invited one to stay for a day or a lifetime. He thought it was kind of strange that the billboard was right on the edge of the cemetery. Someone's idea of a joke or just the Emerald sense of humor?

Following Noel's directions he kept on driving past the sign that pointed west to the business district. His first stop was at Dahlke Enterprises more towards the south part of town, right on the highway.

He had been to Noel's shop in Mason City, and this looked like an upgrade as far as he was concerned. Getting out of his car he looked around to see what Emerald had to offer. What would be his first impression?

It was a clean town and from either direction on the highway, the place looked inviting. There were no trashy areas to speak of and most houses or businesses on the highway were in good shape. He noted Emerald Hydraulics east of town, it looked like a booming business by all the inventory stacked outside and the semis entering and exiting.

Mrs. Stillings saw him standing outside looking around and wondered who he was and where he was going. She got her answer as he headed for the front door.

"Welcome to Dahlke Enterprises. How can I help you?" Mrs. Stillings didn't have time for chit-chat.

He smiled. "Well, good morning." Looking at the nameplate on her desk he continued, "Mrs. Stillings. My name is Mike McCarty and I have an appointment with Noel."

Before she could verify the appointment or buzz him, Noel was out of his office. He recognized the voice. "Hey, Mike! Glad you could make it. Come on in. Could we get you a cup of coffee?"

Mike smiled. "That sounds good but what sounds even better is a restroom."

Noel smiled, "Of course." Mike was pointed in the right direction.

The Grand Tour

"Well, this is all looking very impressive." Mike had just gotten a tour of Jewel Lake. Before that he got a quick glimpse of the business district. Noel wanted him to see not only the town but also the community in general to get the big picture.

"Yeah," Noel said, "and remember, you are probably seeing it at the worst time as winter ends. Just wait until you see it during the other three seasons. On top of that, the two big festivals are Emerald Days in June and Eventide that starts the day after Thanksgiving and runs to Christmas Eve."

Noel parked right next to the place where Mike's shop would be located. Work had already started on sizing down Douglas Hardware to give space to a new business.

"Can we get in to see the amount of space?"

"We sure can." And with that Noel opened the door to a vast area that looked like it was under total reconstruction.

"Nice size area." Mike pictured in his mind what the set-up would look like. Licking his bottom lip a smile started to form.

"So," Noel asked, "what do you think?"

Before Mike could answer Doug Allen said, "Good morning."

Both turned toward the new guy in the shop.

Noel smiled and said, "Hey Doug. Meet Mike McCarty. He might be one of our new business owners. Mike this is Doug Allen, mayor of Emerald."

Eventide

Thanksgiving Day

She checked the thermostat and was happy to see that it needed to be turned up a little. That meant the heat would be coming on. And she could hear it kicking in almost immediately.

This Thanksgiving would be quite different from last year's. She reflected upon all that had happened. Last year her parents stopped on their way down to Corpus Christi for their winter getaway. One might quote Charles Dickens, "It was the best of times. It was the worst of times." Having her parents around was great. They helped with the big reveal in her store. But the other side was that her dad was sick and ultimately, before they made it down to their condo, they stopped at her brother's place. And that brought back all kinds of memories she thought she had buried years ago.

Angela didn't spend a lot of time reflecting on that, just a brief reflection. So many good things had happened this year that they overshadowed all of that. This Thanksgiving would be celebrated like no other. And she was in a very good mood.

Before she got the coffee going she looked outside. The landscape looked barren and even though it wasn't very light out yet, she could tell that the clouds had a solid hold on the sky, just the way she liked it for this time of year.

Time for a shower.

Eventide

Thanksgiving Day—Another Perspective

The covers felt good although they didn't encourage a lot of sleep over the last couple of hours. Her thoughts were all over the place and were getting her nowhere.

She played with the ring on her finger and wondered about the future. She looked forward to it and was scared of it at the same time. Arlene wondered if other women her age and in her situation felt the same way.

Her situation? She had a guy in her life who gave her a Promise

Ring which she accepted with great excitement. The future seemed bright. But now that future was being challenged. Forces outside her control were messing things up. The future she had mapped out in her mind was hitting detours one after another.

We look at other people and they appear to have it altogether, know what they want and go full steam ahead. We assume they know for sure what they want and are on course. What we don't know is that there is not a couple in the world or a specific person that appears that way, that doesn't have doubts or problems.

And what Arlene didn't know was that Brian was feeling somewhat the same way. His love for her was intense and he was willing to do almost anything to get to that point where they would be together for the rest of their lives and raise a family of their own.

Last night was an indication of that love. Knowing that they wouldn't be spending Thanksgiving Day together, they went to the Thanksgiving Eve service at Arlene's church. He wanted to erase any doubts Arlene might have about his feelings for her.

Still, this Thanksgiving morning, Arlene wasn't feeling the peace she wanted to feel.

Spring Break: Easter

As the year progressed, Arlene found herself working more and more hours under the supervision of Michael. It was gradual at first and then a little more intense. Every morning was spent in the studio. The afternoon was free so that she could work at Hakeman's, but some of her evenings she went back to Alcoa to help and learn from Michael's experience.

Arlene found out she had to keep a schedule to know where she had to be at different times. She was busy and she loved it. Time seemed to fly by.

In this busy time, she never forgot about Brian. Her other activities did not interrupt her letter writing. Brian was very important in her mind and in her heart. As the last Friday in March got closer so did her thoughts about her man coming home to her and being with her the next week.

Brian's last class before Spring Break ended at 9:15. And he was ready to get on the road. He had Arlene on his mind in a variety of ways. Yes, he was looking forward to being with her that night. They talked about their first date in what seemed to be years even though it was only weeks. But he also wanted to talk to her about their future. Would he continue at Iowa City? Would he transfer to Alcoa? Would he quit altogether and work somewhere saving up money for them to get married?

You can see that Brian had been doing a lot of thinking. Some of his thoughts may have surprised Arlene. Then again, he might be surprised to hear that she had some of the same questions and even more.

He parks as close to the College Café as he can. He is getting a cup of coffee for the road. In a switch from the way it usually was, Hannah Carpenter is in the booth that they quite often shared. He is surprised to see her there. She doesn't look so happy.

Heading for the door via that booth he says, "Have a great break and a happy Easter!"

As she looks up at him, her eyes are red. He gets the feeling his departure won't go as planned.

Slight Detour

"Hannah! What's wrong?" The concerned look on Brian's face is sincere. He can't just leave her like this. In fact, he wonders if she was just waiting for him to stop by.

She sniffles a little and puts a tissue up to her nose to catch the result of her sorrow. "Everything," she answers. And then she starts to cry a little.

Brian moves into the seat across from her. He just sits there for a while until she gathers herself together. She finally stops crying, pushes her mountain of tissues to the side, and takes a deep breath.

"Kevin and I broke up."

"What?" Brian asks. This is a complete surprise to him. Kevin has been her boyfriend for almost the last two years. She has talked about him on a regular basis. And even though Brian has only seen him a couple times, he still feels he knows him from the way Hannah has talked about him.

"He said he thinks that maybe we need to step back from our ... relationship for a while."

"Where did all this come from?" Brian asks.

"That is what I want to know. I didn't see this coming at all."

Brian asks, "Is there someone else?"

"That's what I asked," Hannah said.

"And..."

"And he said there wasn't. But I think there is."

Brian didn't know what to say. He didn't have to say anything. Hannah just kept on talking about how the breakup took place. He felt bad for her but didn't feel he could leave. And then one of Hannah's girlfriends came in, Dana.

"I just heard." Dana sat down next to Hannah and the waterworks started again.

Brian became a spectator after that. He didn't contribute much but just listened to them talk. He waited there for a half hour before he made his exit. He was anxious to get on the road.

Before he did, Hannah said, "Sorry to dump all this on you but thanks for listening."

He said his good-byes and was off.

Back In Emerald

It was always great to be back in an area he knew so well. And that four-to-five-hour drive didn't seem so bad when he thought about the person he would see when he finally got home. Today he stopped downtown before going home.

Hakeman's always had a different look to it. It depended upon the season, of course. The displays conveyed the feeling of spring and Easter. Everything looked like spring and there was even the sweet smell that spring brings with it.

Angela was the first to see Brian enter. She had been talking to Arlene whose back was to the door. Angela said, "Well, well, look who is back in town."

Arlene looked over her shoulder and was surprised to see Brian. She didn't expect to see him until later. He never surprised her by stopping at the store.

"Brian!" Arlene's eyes lit up as she moved a little faster than usual to greet her guy. She put her arms around him and gave him a big hug.

He whispered into her ear. "It is so good to see you."

She pulled back and looked into his eyes. She wanted to kiss him right then and there but held back. "It is good to see you too." And then the hug changed into them holding hands and asking how long it took to get home and other such meaningless comments.

Angela left them alone to catch up with ... everything. And there were some customers in the store that witnessed the embrace and just smiled.

"When are we going out tonight?" Arlene never stopped smiling. And there was a feeling deep down inside her that she couldn't get rid of, nor did she desire to, just being close to Brian.

Coffee, Cupcakes, and Cream

Everyone in town knew something special was coming. An article in The Emerald Examiner promoted the new business long before opening day. And Mike McCarty took out ads for a few weeks before the opening day to publicize his new place on East Main.

But not everyone was so sure about the added store. Emerald, the NEW Emerald, had been in existence for almost ten years and most of the stores were redeveloped old stores. This guy was really someone no one knew about, except for Noel Dahlke.

Now you might think that because he had an automatic seal of approval by Noel that he would be accepted without a second thought. But people can be funny and unpredictable at times. And this was one of those times.

And since Douglas Hardware sacrificed a good deal of their square footage for Coffee, Cupcakes, and Cream to enter the business district, well, that was a little suspicious too. You wouldn't think the people of Emerald would be that way, but some were.

Still, just in the construction of the new business, foot traffic increased as people ventured to see what was going on. Time would tell whether this would be a success or not.

In bringing in this new business Noel thought there would be interest in other businesses in following Carl's lead. But it wasn't happening as fast as he thought it would. Some things just take time.

Bonnie's Café

"Well, what do you think of the new addition to the downtown?" Ginger asked and then took a bite of her pie.

"You mean that ice cream place?" Anita asked.

"Yeah. It looks pretty impressive."

"It does. Better than I thought it would. At first, when I saw how the hardware store had to cram things together, I wasn't sure. Not that I go in there a lot by any means. Jeff said it looks better than it did before."

"Fred said the same thing. So have you been IN the new store yet?"

"No I haven't. But Emily has and she really likes it. She has tried several flavors and has a card with three stars on it already."

"What does that mean?"

Anita said, "I guess it means that when she gets ten stars she gets something free. Not a bad gimmick."

"We should go over there sometime."

"Yeah, we should."

Pop's Pizza

They decided that Friday night would just be the time to meet at Pop's. After all, it had been a long drive for Brian, and this would be a little more casual. Arlene didn't mind. Saturday night would be more dress up and they had all next week to be together.

They sat across from one another, holding hands across the table, waiting for their pizza.

"I can't believe you are here. I have missed you so much." Arlene's eyes sparkled as she was almost on the verge of tearing up, so happy that Brian was home.

He squeezed her hand. "I know. I feel the same." And then he rubbed the finger on which the Promise Ring was very prominent.

Looking into her eyes he said, "I have lots to talk to you about."

At one time that might have frightened Arlene, hearing those words. But not anymore. Just the way he said what he did gave her goosebumps.

"Oh, really," she coyly smiled. "Like what?"

He looked up and said, "Oh, I don't know, maybe our future." And then he looked into her eyes.

"What about our future?" She bit her bottom lip.

Before anything more could be said, their pizza arrived, and the conversation got more casual for a while. Brian listened to Arlene as she talked about photography and all she had learned. He loved to hear her talk and how she got excited about things.

He looked at her and wondered how every time he saw her she looked different, prettier, more mature. And he wondered how he was so lucky to be with her.

The pizza they got was a medium and didn't take long to eat. Pop's was starting to get crowded and a little noisier. They were about to leave when Jared and Brenda entered.

"Mind if we join you?"

"Not at all!" Brian got into Arlene's side of the booth and Arlene didn't budge an inch. She liked the feel of Brian sitting next to her. Any more discussion about their future was put on hold for now.

Eventide

The First Friday

Everything was going according to plan. The lights throughout all the downtown were off giving an eerie feeling but a feeling of anticipation as well. Eventide was about to begin. This rehearsed beginning was getting better each year.

First, all the lights everywhere downtown were turned off. Then the tree in the middle of Memorial Park would be lit, 'O Christmas Tree' would be introduced by a soloist or ensemble of some kind. Then the rest of the Christmas lights came on and stores revealed how they decorated for the festival.

Inside Hakeman's they were ready, and a replay of the previous year took place. In the darkness that preceded the official beginning, the partition separating the grand display was moved to the side for people to witness what was offered this year.

Extra help had been hired to help with the crowds they were expecting. Noel was on hand and had become quite familiar with retail. He had spent a lot of this week helping to make sure everything went off without a hitch. It seemed like all was going according to plan.

Arlene was also on hand but didn't have Brian standing next to her like she did last year. And that was a little strange, although you couldn't tell that from her demeanor. She had a big smile on her face, dressed in a way that exuded Eventide and gave a look that made other young women long to be like her and made young men wonder if she was available or not.

At the end of the evening when the door was locked, all the employees took a moment to sit down in the back and talk about the experience they had just ... had.

"Wow. I didn't think it could get any better than it did last year. But I think it did!" Shirley was the first to make a comment.

Noel was rubbing his face. He looked tired. "I know what you mean. I only worked one night last year and ... I don't know... I think you need to hire more help for next year... or maybe even next week!"

Sitting next to hm, Angela rubbed his back. "I have never seen you so tired. Thanks for helping out so much."

One person who didn't look a bit tired was Arlene. "Well, is it okay if I take off?"

"Hot date?" Noel smiled and was joined by everyone else.

Arlene gave half a smile. "Something like that."

"See you tomorrow," Angela said.

And Arlene was out the door.

Brian's Thoughts

As Arlene and Brian didn't get to end the night the way they thought they would, Brian did not have the time to talk to Arlene about his thoughts and plans for the summer. The summer break between his first and second year of college would be one that included him finding work... somewhere. And that somewhere had to be in the Emerald area.

He had two choices, as he saw it. He could work at Fitzgerald

Manufacturing. There weren't a whole lot of employees there, but he didn't need any special skills either. He knew students who had worked there before, and it didn't seem like a bad place to work. You got pretty dirty at times but who cares, it is still a job and more important, it is a paycheck.

The other place he was considering was Emerald Hydraulics. They employed a lot of part-time summer help. Employees, by in large, took most of their vacations during the summer. You always needed to find someone to fill in. And here, too, you were more valuable if you had some skills with one of the machines, but there were also areas where you were just the "grunt" that could be moved here or there where needed. He didn't care if they looked at him that way. Once again, it was a paycheck.

In both cases he would be around Emerald and most important of all, he would be around Arlene. Well, employment was one of the things they would talk about tonight. But there were other things as well.

Alone Together At Last

Arlene was okay with Brenda and Jared butting in at Pop's. Not that she didn't want some alone time with Brian, but it was okay. It had been a long day for both of them.

You kind of wonder sometimes what makes a long day… a long day. It was easy to see it from Brian's point of view with the long drive and all. But what about Arlene's point of view? Well, the simple truth is that when you are waiting for someone and can't wait to see them, sometimes that can be exhausting too. And you don't realize it is happening.

Tonight they went to Alcoa, ate at the mall, and took their time walking around, hand in hand, just enjoying being with one another.

"You know, this is kind of fun." Arlene looked at Brian, smiled, squeezed his hand.

Brian returned her smile. "Yeah, I thought it might be. Being anywhere with you is fun. It has been way too long." Their stroll kind of perturbed some of those wanting others to walk a little faster. But these two didn't even notice.

"How long before school gets out for you?" Arlene was curious.

"I think it is the middle of May. Something like that. Maybe a little later. How about you?"

"The same, I think. I don't know if I will have to work more with Michael or not. We haven't talked about that a whole lot."

On their walk they noticed a number of other couples walking. Most were hand in hand. But there were some who were also pushing a stroller. Arlene was the one that noticed and thought to herself, "They look pretty young to have a baby."

Brian didn't notice them at all. He had something he wanted to share with Arlene. "While I am home for this week I was thinking of applying for work at a couple of places."

"Oh, really?"

"Yeah. Need a lot of money to make sure that my girl … well, I want to keep her happy." He gave a sly grin.

"Oh, I don't know," Arlene said without even looking at him. "Why don't you just take her for a walk in the park or at the mall? That is a pretty cheap date." She looked at him and then continued. "Besides, I don't think she expects a lot. She probably just likes being with her guy."

They both enjoyed this conversation and felt the love.

College Plans

"Are you planning on going back to Iowa City in the fall?"

"That is another thing I want to take a closer look at. I want to talk to one of the admission counselors about transferring my credits to Alcoa, if I can, and then looking into journalism there."

"Really?" Arlene was excited hearing Brian's plans. He was actually going to do it. "That sounds great. I hope it all works out."

"Yeah, I hope so too."

And then Arlene brought up something she had never brought up before. "How do your parents feel about you NOT going back to Iowa City?"

"Well..." Brian was slow in responding. "They don't actually know about that yet."

"You haven't told them."

He scrunched his face a little. "Uh... not exactly."

"Why?"

"I don't know. I know I have to sometime but... I don't know what they will say." Brian looked up at nothing for a moment and then went on. "I mean, I know they will think that I am transferring because of you."

"And that will be a bad thing?"

"I didn't say that. It is just that... well... maybe they are thinking that we are getting a little too serious too soon."

Arlene looked down and then hesitantly asked. "Is that what you think?"

"No. No. Not at all." And then just to be on the safe side, Brian asked, "Do you... uh... think we are?"

"I don't know. I don't think so."

They both looked down as they walked along. This conversation kind of had a turn that neither expected.

They had just reached Younkers and the shop next to it offered ice cream. "Want to share a Sundae?" Brian asked.

They sat down and quietly started in on the dessert.

"Arlene. What I said,,.. it doesn't mean... I mean I still love you."

"And I still love you."

They played with one another's fingers. A smile was shared. Such serious talk was not going to spoil their night. And with that they really didn't care about the ice cream anymore.

Wedding Plans

The news that Noel and Angela were engaged was greeted by many as FINALLY. Many times in the past, people thought they were headed for the altar, which is what Angela had guessed as well until Noel was a no-show for one reason or another. But now it was official. Their picture was in the Examiner and an expected June wedding was also assumed.

And the two lovebirds were seen together quite a bit. Even though his office was on the highway, he spent a lot of time downtown, specifically in Hakeman's.

It was a slow morning. For some reason people seemed to be avoiding the downtown. Everyone wondered what was going on. As it turned out, nothing special was going on. There was no conspiracy to avoid shopping. By the afternoon that would all change. But right now, taking a break is very easy.

Shirley poured herself a cup of coffee and sat down in the back room with an eye on the door in case someone should enter. Really didn't have to do that as the bell would signal someone's entry.

"So, how are the wedding plans going?" She looked Angela's way with a bored smile on her face.

With raised eyebrows Angela looked up from her paperwork, which was also getting tiresome. "Well, pretty good, I guess. Got the invitations just the other day."

"You invite a lot of people?"

"Yeah, I suppose we did. Noel's family is really big into ... about everything it seems. More people coming from his side than mine."

And more discussion took place about where the reception was going to be and when the wedding shower would take place. And then they were interrupted as they were everyday about this time.

"Hey, Ange, you around?"

"Back here Noel." She really didn't have to say it. Before she was finished, he had already walked in.

He bent over and gave her a kiss as she stayed seated.

"Got some honeymoon options to show you."

"You do?"

Shirley perked up. "Oh, that sounds exciting." And then she asked, "Who is going to run the store while you are gone?"

Angela looked at her and slowly said, "Well, I thought that between you and Arlene, you could handle it." Angela waited for an answer but getting none she asked, "Can't you?"

A Fast Week

They had been spoiled by the break at Christmas that lasted for three whole weeks. Spring break flew by way too fast. Still, Arlene and Brian spent a lot of time together. Most of the time was not on what you would call a formal date. Instead they were at either Brian's place or Arlene's.

Whenever they went out to Pop's they would be joined by Brenda and Jared at some point. And they didn't mind that. The four really enjoyed being together.

"When do you have to leave?" Jared was the one asking the question.

Brian took a deep breath before answering. He looked over at Arlene as if she were asking the question. "No sooner than I have too." Then he looked at Jared. "Maybe three Sunday afternoon. I am in no rush to get back to Iowa City."

Brenda looked at Arlene and then Brian, "The sooner you leave, the sooner you will get back."

"That makes no sense." Arlene quipped.

Brenda shrugged her shoulders. "I was just trying to put a positive spin on Brian getting back here when school was out."

"I know." Arlene said. "And I appreciate it."

"Hey, I haven't left yet. Let's enjoy the time we have. Come on guys let's liven things up."

Jared smiled, "That's the spirit. What should we do?"

Nobody said anything. Then they decided to order a pizza.

Sunday Afternoon

He was packed up and would be heading out soon but right now he was going to spend time with Arlene. Around two he picked her up. "Let's go for a drive."

They walked down the steps from her front porch. She scooted in on the driver's side. She was still wearing her new Easter dress.

"That dress is really pretty."

"Well, thank you," she said. "I was hoping you would like it."

"And your perfume is driving me crazy!"

"Good! I don't want you to be distracted by any of those coeds down in Iowa City."

"Oh, I won't be. I have your picture front and center in my room."

"Good."

"And I talk about you so much that people are getting bored with it."

"I hope you're not." Arlene said with raised eyebrows.

"Never!" And before he started the car he took the opportunity to give her an extended kiss. She didn't mind as he pulled her close.

Leaving her house they drove through downtown and just happened to see Jake and Rachael walking toward Memorial Park. As Arlene saw what Rachael was wearing, she thought to herself that the dress she (Arlene) had was much prettier. The two were still friends but, sometimes Arlene saw her as competition.

State Park

This was turning out to be a beautiful Easter! Hardly a cloud in the sky. A soft breeze made it seem a little chillier than it actually was. A coat would feel good, but Arlene didn't have one. She didn't mind getting closer to Brian. And while they were holding hands at first, as they walked down to the lake, his arm was around her.

People were scarce in the park this time of year. In a couple of months it will be different. Memorial Day will bring the crowds and by the Fourth of July the beach will have a lot of activity.

But right now, these two are thinking only of the minutes ticking by before Brian is on the Interstate and further and further from Arlene.

"I look forward to the time when you don't have to go to Iowa City anymore." Arlene laid her head on his shoulder.

"Me, too." Brian said. Pulling her close, he gave out a sigh. Then he rubbed her arm and said, "Even though I can hardly wait to be home after this semester is over and be with you more often, I also think beyond that and what our future will be like."

"Do you? I mean do you really think about that?"

"Yes, I do. In my mind I am wondering about a lot of things." He looked at her. "And you are the center of them all."

"What do you wonder about?" And now Arlene is standing directly in front of him, holding his hands and looking into his eyes.

Brian pursed his lips, looked up at the sky and then into her eyes. "I wonder about how long it will have to be before we can be together all the time. And I wonder if going back to school and all... well... should I or shouldn't I ... I don't know."

And thinking that he was talking about marriage she hugged him very tightly before saying, "I wonder about a lot of things, too.

But there is one thing I don't wonder about."

"What's that?"

"Loving you." And after that there was a kiss and the talking ended. It was time to head back to Iowa City.

Wedding Preparations

Angela was able to get wedding invitations at a fabulous price, being in the business as she was. Still, the number of invitations seemed to be staggering. Noel didn't give it a thought. Financially, they seemed to live in different worlds. But that would all soon change.

This was a topic of discussion between Noel and Angela at various times as they planned their future.

"Well, I would suggest that you don't change the name of the store." Noel said with raised eyebrows.

"But I won't be a Hakeman anymore. I will be a Dahlke." Angela replied with her mouth open a little as she played with Noel. She liked the sound of Angela Dahlke.

"You bet you will be a Dahlke." Noel gave a big grin, "But it is a good business practice to leave the name the same. People are familiar with it and... it kind of has a ... nostalgic ring to it. Don't you think?"

"You're going to change the name of the store?" Shirley heard a little of the conversation in the back room as she got to work on Monday morning.

"Probably not," Angela smiled. "We were just talking about wedding plans -and that came up.

"I never thought about that being a possibility. When people heard that Hakeman's was coming back, I think they kind of liked that, even though it wasn't the Hakeman's of the past." Since there was no response from the other two, Shirley dropped the subject.

"Well," Noel said, "I gotta get going Ange. Stretch Odiot is waiting for me, and I suppose I better get over to the Coopers before they fire me." A quick kiss and he was gone.

Unexpected Offer

The morning was filled with surprises. Arlene's morning was filled with activities at the studio. She had just found out that her time with Michael would come to a close at the end of the semester. Some budget thing with the college was the reason.

"Sorry to hear about the change," Michael said. "I was looking forward to spending a little more time with you."

Arlene sighed, "Well, I have enjoyed working with you. You have taught me a lot. I can't believe how much I've learned in such a short period of time."

"Well, you are a good learner and I think you have a future in photography. Are you planning on opening your own studio?"

This was a surprise question as far as Arlene was concerned. "I don't really know. In fact, you know, you have taught me a lot about photography, but I wouldn't know where to start doing something like that. In fact, that seems kind of scary."

Michael sat there for a minute and then asked, "Arlene, would you like to work for me after the semester is over?"

"Work for you?"

"Yes. I could use the extra help and ... maybe I could show you a little more about the business end of doing things. And... well, we could see where it goes from there. What do you think?"

"Wow!" Arlene was surprised at the offer. "I don't know. That is a lot to think about." She sat there just thinking about the possibilities. "Can I think about it?"

"Sure. Sure. No rush. Let me know whenever you decide. Would like to help you out and you would be helping me out as well."

Unexpected News

Arlene usually spent most of her driving time thinking about Brian, Hakeman's, or photography. Okay, most of the time it was about Brian. But on her way home today, all she could think about was the offer Michael had given her. How did she feel about that? She didn't know. She truly didn't know. Working for Michael was a big step. And it meant that she really needed to decide where this whole photography thing was going.

The thirty miles back to Emerald seemed to go by like a flash. No sooner had she parked across from Hakeman's facing Memorial Park, but Brenda ran across the street and grabbed her. "I have something to tell you."

Brenda took her by the arm, and they went over to the shelter house where they both sat down.

Arlene looked a little perturbed at her best friend and asked, "So what's up?"

"You'll never guess."

"Guess what?"

"What happened yesterday."

"What happened yesterday?"

Brenda looked around as if to see if anyone else was listening. She got close to Arlene and took her time spitting it out. “Someone got a ring!”

Arlene’s jaw dropped. “Jared proposed to you?” And then she looked down at Brenda’s hand.

“No, he didn’t.” Brenda didn’t say anything for a while. “But someone else did.”

“Who then?” Arlene looked puzzled.

“I don’t know if I should tell you.”

“Why?”

“I don’t know how you will take it.”

They both sat there for a moment. And then the light bulb went on. Arlene looked at Brenda. “Was it Rachael? Did Jake ask ... did he propose to Rachael?”

Brenda said nothing, just nodded her head. She wasn’t sure how Arlene ... what she would say or do.

“Wow!” Arlene said.

Brenda looked at her. “You okay?”

Arlene didn’t answer for a while. “Yeah. Yeah, I’m okay. It just took me by surprise.”

“You sure?”

Arlene wrinkled her nose. “Yeah, I’m sure. I had thoughts that might be coming. And since I have Brian... I don’t know. It really doesn’t bother me. Kind of surprises me too. When did he ask her?"

"Yesterday afternoon, I guess."

"Was it here in the shelter house?"

"I don't know. Why would you say that?"

"Because Brian and I were driving past here, and I saw them together. Who would have thought?"

Shirley

She enjoyed working at Hakeman's even though or possibly because it was basically just half-days. Most of the time she was home by noon and had the rest of the day to do... things.

Shirley enjoyed being involved in the lives of Angela and Arlene. And by being involved it meant basically keeping up with what was happening. Between the two of them there was always something going on and plans for the future were abundant, or so it seemed.

The age difference between them all almost made it seem like three generations and in a way it was close. Shirley was close to the same age as Angela's mom and if you scrunched the numbers enough she was also old enough to be Arlene's grandmother.

Shirley had excellent hearing as well. When she sensed

something was very personal or intimate in nature, she would give each their space. Although she didn't get too far away. She wanted to hear what was going on. And most of the time she did.

But while her hearing was superb, something else appeared to not be quite as good. It happened shortly after Easter, while putting away merchandise in preparation for the next holiday, Shirley happened to fall.

Angela was in the back room and heard some commotion. There were customers shopping and she didn't know what happened. She came out immediately to find Shirley on the floor, a very embarrassed Shirley at that.

"What happened?"

Shirley pushed herself up a little. "I don't know. I guess I tripped on something. Don't know what it could have been."

A customer shared, "I saw her walking out of the corner of my eye and then, all of a sudden, there was this crash."

"Glad I didn't take down the crystal display." It was next to where she was. It rattled a little as Shirley hit the floor. "Clumsy me."

Shirley had help getting up. She brushed herself off, made sure her hair was okay and got back to work. Embarrassing.

It would happen again.

Talking with the Folks

"Do you know the date for the shower?" Joanie asked.

"It is supposed to be..." Angela was looking through her calendar. "Uh, May...19th."

"That a Sunday?"

"...Yes. It is a Sunday afternoon. You think you will be able to come down?"

"Planning on it. Is that okay?"

"Oh, sure. Bring Dad with you."

"Of course. I wouldn't drive that far without him."

"You doing okay Mom?" Arlene thought she heard a little scare in her mom's voice.

"Yes, yes. Everything is fine. I am so happy for you Angela. Are you getting excited?"

"Yes, I am. It is going to be a big step. But it is the right step." And then she thought about something. "Oh, and thanks for sending the addresses down for the invitations."

"Have you looked at them yet?"

"No. Just opened the envelope and saw what they were. It is something Noel and I will have to get busy on."

"Well," Joanie said, "these were just the suggestions we had of people that we thought should be at your wedding. You can decide if you want them there or not."

"I'm sure the list will be okay."

More chit-chat continued before they hung up. But this conversation will continue and not be as pleasant in the near future.

Back on Campus

Hannah Carpenter didn't enjoy the Easter break very much. When she and Kevin broke up, that seemed to change everything. And that included driving back and forth from Davenport. They each had their own vehicles but when they were a couple, Kevin usually drove, and they left Hannah's car in Iowa City. It was a sad, lonely, and long week for Hannah. She was looking forward to getting back to school.

When Brian pulled into the parking lot close to his dorm, he felt relieved to be back at school. At least the long drive was over. And maybe it was for good, depending on whether he would be attending there in the fall.

Thinking about his future, their future, his and Arlene's, kept his mind going the whole 5 hours he traveled. He looked forward to a good 8 hours of sleep before he hit the road running the next morning.

His first class he could have skipped. Boring and repetitive. Maybe the prof didn't want to be there any more than the students. Brian picked up on his old habit of going to the College Café for coffee and maybe something to eat.

Not a whole lot of students were sitting around this morning. But he did see someone he knew, sitting where he usually sat. And for that matter, it seemed where she usually sat as well. There was Hannah.

"Well, how did Easter break go for you?" he asked.

She looked up. No red puffy eyes. But no smile either. Just a forlorn look. "Okay, I guess... considering."

"Nothing changed between you and Kevin? I mean, you still aren't going together anymore."

"No. Didn't see him once during the break. We were inseparable at Christmas and now nothing."

Brian rubbed his cheeks and said, "I am so sorry about all this. Can't imagine what you are going through." Then he waited for her to say something.

But before she could, Dana came over and sat down next to her. "How's it going Hannah?" This was the first time they had seen each other since the break.

It wasn't long before Brian got the feeling he was the third wheel in this ... whatever it was. But he stayed for a while. To leave would have seemed awkward. When he thought he had stayed long enough he made his excuses as he got up to leave.

"Thanks for being here," Hannah looked at him before he got up. She put her hand over his and gave him a look. He wasn't sure what that meant. Probably nothing.

The Ring

She told Brenda that the ring Rachael received, her engagement ring didn't really bother her. And it didn't. She didn't think it did. But she wasn't really sure.

It is not that she had designs on Jake yet, or anything like that. She wasn't even jealous of Rachael at this point. She had gotten over that completely.

And she didn't have doubts about Brian either. She knew they were on the same page regarding their relationship. She was certain of that. So why couldn't she get her mind on something other than the fact that Jake and Rachael were engaged?

She decided she needed to talk this all through with her best friend, Brenda. And that is why they were sitting together out at

Pop's Pizza on this weeknight, just the two of them.

"How close are you and Jared to getting married?"

"What?"

"Are you and Jared getting close to getting married?"

"I don't know. Why this concern about me and Jared?"

Arlene sighed and looked to the side. "I don't know. Ever since Jake and Rachael got engaged, I don't know... I am happy for them, but..."

"Okay."

"But... I don't think I am jealous of them, or what. But it has been bugging me."

Brenda got closer to Arlene. "Have you got the bug ..."

"The bug?"

"You know. Do you want to get engaged now too?"

"Oh!" Arlene scorned the thought or idea. But then she said, "I don't know. I don't think so. But I don't know."

Silence.

Then Brenda said, "Well, Jared and I have talked about it, and we were kind of thinking about getting married ourselves, sooner than later. But then Jake proposed... out of the blue... and we didn't want to steal his ... their thunder. You know what I mean?"

"Yes and no. I didn't know you were that close to getting engaged."

"I guess we'll never know."

"Have Jake and Rachael set a date yet?"

"Sometime in September, I think."

Arlene thought talking with Brenda might help. But it didn't.

Eventide

After Closing

"Well, how did tonight go? Was it a madhouse like last year?" Brian asked Arlene as she got in his car. Since he was picking her up, she got in on the passenger side but wasted no time scooting over.

"It was unbelievable." That was all Arlene said at first. But that was also after a kiss she initiated. "The whole night it was customer after customer."

"Did Angela have enough help?"

"I don't think so. Then again, the lines weren't that long that often."

"Was Shirley working the other checkout line?"

"Yeah, she was."

"How did she do?"

"Okay, I guess. I think she was pretty wiped out after tonight."

"Do you think it was because of..."

"I don't know what to think. But let's not talk any more about that. Let's talk about us. Okay?"

He pulled her close and she leaned her head on his shoulder. "You want to go for a ride?"

"I don't care. I just want to be with you. Wherever you are or go, I want to be with you."

They both were facing a problem they didn't expect. How it would be resolved, neither knew.

Addressing Invitations

"How many addresses do we have Ange?" Noel asked.

Angela took out the papers she received from her parents and then the number Noel's mom sent. "Don't know for sure but it looks like a lot." She laid the stack on the dining room table.

"That it does." Noel said. He flipped through the pile.

“You know what I think would be a good idea?” Angela said.

“What?”

“You address the ones to your side, and I will do the same from my side.” She had a smile on her face as Noel’s side was considerably longer.

“Oh, no!” Noel answered. “We are in this together.”

“I was just kidding. But we better get started. It is going to be a long afternoon.”

And it would be. But the time went fast as with almost every address they would talk about why this person was being invited or how that person had an impact in their life and so on. After about an hour it was time for a break.

“Hey, Noel, how come I have more invitations done than you do?”

“I don’t know.”

“I do.”

“Why?”

“Because you are a slacker. That is why.”

Noel smiled. “Am not.”

“Yes you are.”

“Am not.”

“Get your own lemonade. Meet you out on the porch swing.”

Noel sat down and gave out a huge sigh. "Think we'll get done today?"

"Don't know. Hope so."

Silence for a while.

"I like your place Ange."

She looked over at him. "Do you really?" They had talked about where they would live after they got married. She got the feeling Noel would want to live in a nicer place, a bigger place.

"Yes, I do. I like it's location, the size, almost everything about it."

"That surprises me. Is this going to be our home, then?"

"If that is okay with you." Noel looked at her.

Well, living in her house would be okay with Angela as she thought about it now. But something Noel innocently did, just minutes ago, would not!

What Was That All About?

As Brian left the College Café and headed toward his next class he happened to glance back through the window next to the booth he just left. As fate would have it, he saw Hannah looking at him. He quickly dismissed the gaze and moved along.

He also hoped that Dana would be able to help Hannah with her problems. While he sympathized with Hannah and her situation, he knew better than to get involved any deeper with her. Especially after that look. This could get complicated and ... it could get messy.

Arlene didn't like the fact that she gave Brian a note... of any kind. He was not about to jeopardize his relationship with Arlene. Hannah had her problems. And while they became ... friendly with one another... that was it.

He even thought that maybe he should try to talk with Kevin and see what happened. But not knowing him or what he was like, he shied away from any contact. No, he was not going to let Hannah's problem become HIS problem. Hannah and Dana can figure this out.

But try as he may, he couldn't get that look out of his mind, the look Hannah gave. He didn't dwell on it. But still...

Stepchild Studio

With a click of the camera and taking a last look at how the shot went, Michael said, "Well, that does it. Looks really good."

"How soon will we be able to see proofs?" Typical question for two people who just got engaged. And the question was asked by the bride-to-be rather than the other half.

"I would think... maybe a week. That soon enough?" Michael couldn't help smiling back. She had taken a lot of engagement pictures and was involved in many of the same weddings.

"Sounds good to us." The couple joined hands and headed for the door.

Arlene was watching the two. She surmised that they were probably about her age. They were from Pocahontas, a few miles north of Emerald. She didn't know anything about them but envied them and their plans.

"Arlene, Arlene. You seem to know what I want done before I do at times. You have really become invaluable to me. Do you know that?" Michael was looking in her direction as she sat down to rest with a cup of coffee.

Arlene was busy putting some of the equipment away. "Well, you are easy to work for, that is for sure, and I've enjoyed my time here."

"Have you given any thought to my proposal?"

"You mean about working for you?" Then a pause. "I have. But that is a tough one."

And then they both looked toward the door. The people who entered weren't customers.

Arlene knew one of the two.

"Hey Mom." Daniel was the first to say anything.

The girl, woman, with him was the same blonde Arlene saw weeks ago. At least she thought she was. Her hair was styled perfectly. Her make-up, impeccable.

Michael asked, “Where did you pick her up?”

“Just got back from Urbandale. Lisa had a shoot for that new beauty salon.” And then looking towards Arlene, he said, “Arlene. Right?”

“You’ve got a good memory.” Arlene was surprised that after just one time working together and that being a while back, that Daniel remembered her.

“Arlene, this is my sister, Lisa.” And then looking toward Lisa he said, “Lisa this is Arlene… I don’t know your last name.”

“Plummer.”

“Plummer. She goes to the college and Mom is helping her learn the trade.”

“Nice to meet you Arlene.” Lisa was as nice and polite as you would expect her to be.

“Nice meeting you as well.” Arlene was taken with Lisa, and she immediately wondered if she had seen Lisa in any commercials. “You are very pretty. Do you do a lot of commercials?”

Lisa blushed a little and answered, “Not as many as I would like. The competition is pretty tough out there. But thanks to Mom and Daniel, my name and my face are getting out there more and more.”

And family talk took over after that. Arlene was glad because she didn't know what answer to give to Michael about working for her. As far as Arlene was concerned, a lot of things were still... up in the air.

Stretch Odiot

While Stretch Odiot had a Buddy Hackett smile many associated with him, as far as Noel was concerned, Stretch reminded him of an actor who played in a lot of westerns, Slim Pickens. He never was a star, but you saw him as being a sidekick a lot.

Noel was trying to get him set up with a person Noel knew who wanted to expand his television and stereo business. Noel had the idea that Stretch could give the new guy space just like Douglas Hardware gave space to Mike McCarty for his ice cream and coffee endeavor.

Stretch was never in too much of a rush on things. But he had seen the foot traffic pick up on his side of the street, so it looked like Noel's endeavors were pretty successful.

"Uh, this guy you got in mind, just how old is he?"

Noel wasn't expecting this question. "Well, I don't really know how old he is, but he has had a lot of experience in the business."

"He has, huh?"

"Yeah. He and his older brother have a pretty good business going up in Spencer. I think he is interested in seeing what he can do on his own."

"Okay. Okay. I can see that. Can I meet him sometime?"

"I'm sure you can. He is a pretty nice guy. And I think he will be good working with more of a younger crowd. He just has that look." Noel went on, "Let me see when he might be available."

"Good enough. I'll wait till I hear from you."

Noel headed to the office to make the connection.

What's Going On?

Arlene was a little late coming back from Alcoa, so Shirley stayed later than usual at Hakeman's. For some reason things picked up at a time of day they didn't usually. Angela could use the extra help.

Shirley was bringing the last picture frame they had with a military theme focusing on Memorial Day. Someone had sold the one on display and it hadn't been replaced. "This is the last one, Doris. Didn't think we had any left. Glad I looked in back."

"Thank you so much Shirley. This will be perfect. I have wanted to display a picture of my Dad when he came home from his tour in Viet Nam." Her Dad died earlier in the year. This would be the first Memorial Day his name would be read at the cemetery.

After handing the frame to Doris, Shirley turned around but in so doing that, she fell flat on the floor. Fortunately, she didn't hit any of the displays as she was in the section where there was a lot of crystal.

Doris asked, "Are you okay, Shirley?"

Angela heard the fall and came right over. "Shirley, everything alright?"

Shirley tried to push herself up but was having a problem doing that. "I don't know. Something doesn't seem to be working here."

Both Doris and Angela tried to help her up, but something was wrong. Shirley wasn't really helping. It wasn't because she didn't want to. It was because she couldn't. With Doris holding on to her, Angela brought out a chair for Shirley.

"What happened?" Angela asked.

Shirley rubbed her head. "I don't know. I went to move my legs and they wouldn't move." She tried to move them now and they seemed to work fine.

"You know, I had the same problem a few days ago. I wonder what is wrong. Maybe I should see Dr. Floyd."

Angela said, "I think that would be a good idea. See what he has to say. Probably nothing. But get it checked out."

The bell above the door signaled someone new in the store.

"What's going on?" Arlene just entered.

Angela explained what happened.

Before leaving Doris asked, "I will help you down to The Clinic if you want."

"Thanks but I think I will wait. Things seem to be working fine right now." And then turning to Angela, "All right if I leave now?"

"Sure. Do you want me to take you home?"

"No. I will be okay."

And everyone watched as she went to her car and took off.

Iowa City

Brian didn't know what to do. This was kind of getting out of hand. His chance meeting with Hannah at the College Café was turning into an every morning activity. He didn't mind it when she would on occasion sit and talk with him but this every morning routine, well, it didn't work for him.

And on top of that, even though she would talk about Kevin a lot, he also got the feeling that she was getting closer to him. And he didn't need that. She knew he had a girlfriend but that didn't seem to matter. Was she doing this on purpose? Or did she not even realize what was happening? Hopefully, the latter.

So far on this particular morning, she was a no show. And just so that he had made it clear that he and Arlene were a couple, he brought the last two love letters she sent. Well, that wasn't the only reason. The last two she sent were kind of steaming with passion. He didn't mind reading them over and over again.

He looked at his watch and hoped Hannah was a no show as she hadn't come in yet. He was about to leave when he heard a knock on the window. It was Hannah.

"I know I am late, but can we talk for just a minute?"

"Sure. Sure."

"Great! I will be right back."

It was getting close to the time he had to leave. Finally getting back to the booth she sat down and said, "I heard from Kevin."

"You did?"

"Yeah. He wants to talk."

"That sounds great." Brian started to feel relief.

"Well, I don't know."

"What do you mean, you don't know?"

"Well, I was sad at first but now I am kind of getting angry at him for what he has put me through."

"Don't you think you better talk to him first and find out what he has to say?"

Hannah thought for a minute. "Maybe I do." And then she got real serious, "But it better be good. I think I am ready to move on."

As they talked a little more, Brian didn't know if he was relieved or not. Then again, the school year was close to ending and then he thought he would be done with this whole scenario. "Well let me know what happens." But as he said that he was hoping she wouldn't. He was really hoping he would never have to hear anything about these two again.

Mother's Day

Vera Plummer was very happy about the gift her daughter got her for Mother's Day. "That is so nice. You are so thoughtful, Arlene."

"Well," she smiled, "I work at the best place in town, and they had all kinds of wonderful things to pick from." That was true. And even before items were put on display or cards were slid into their slots, Arlene had the opportunity to choose what she wanted to give her Mom.

She was spending all of Sunday afternoon with her. She and her Mom got along very well although they weren't extremely close. She was more of a "Daddy's" girl. But Vera didn't mind.

They were sitting on the sun porch enjoying the gorgeous spring day. "Mom, can I ask you a question?"

"Certainly."

"Before you and Dad got married, well how long did you know him?"

Vera had been wondering if this question would ever come up. She had an idea that Arlene and Brian were getting serious. And when those feelings started it was going to be hard to pull in the reins on their feelings for one another.

"Well," she thought for a moment, "I guess it was a couple of years or so."

"When did you know that he was the one?"

"Oh, that is a good question." Vera bit her bottom lip a little before answering. "I don't know. I had doubts at various times. Neither of us dated a lot back in those days." And then trying to change the subject she asked, "Why do you ask? Does it have anything to do with you and Brian? Are you getting serious?"

Arlene looked away. She didn't want to say how crazy she was about Brian. She wanted to appear more mature. "I don't know." She rubbed her Promise Ring which Vera noticed. "It is just that it feels so right about being with him."

"It felt right being with Jake, too, didn't it?" Vera asked and then wished she hadn't.

"But that was different." Arlene got a little defensive. "Jake ... being with Jake was good for a while. But then everything fell apart. And now he has Rachael, and they seem to be perfect together."

And then it got quiet for a little bit.

Arlene quietly spoke again. "I just feel really close to Brian. And he feels the same about me. After all, he gave me this Promise Ring." She looked down at it and played with it a little.

"Well," Vera said, "I don't know what to say. You will have to make up your own mind about him... about the two of you. Whatever you decide... you are old enough to make your own decisions although you are always going to be my little girl."

"I know Mom."

"Talk to me anytime."

"I will."

Vera wanted to say more but thought it best not to at this time. Still she wondered about all that was happening and how fast it seemed to be happening. Then again, was she much different at Arlene's age?

The Last Day

Only one more day and he would be out of there. Back to Emerald. Back to Arlene. And possibly never to be apart from her again! He had one more test to take and then he would be through with Iowa City.

He had his car packed with all his earthly possessions. It was packed to the gills. He had just enough room to squeeze in behind the wheel. He left a little hole in the floor to ceiling stash to be able to use his rear-view mirror. And that was it.

He risked going to the College Café. He was hoping he had seen Hannah for the last time. Fortunately she never showed up. He thought to himself, "I hope she is back with Kevin, that everything is rosy in their lives, and they will live happily ever after."

The café was not very busy, and he did a little bit of last-minute studying, although he didn't think the test would be that bad. He finished his coffee and took off toward the building where the class was held.

Walking through campus there was a feeling of freedom. There was not the casual walking around you usually saw. People were moving with a purpose and that purpose was not to grow in knowledge but to get out of Dodge!

Finishing the test, he felt good about how he had done. Maybe not the best grade but far from the worst. And he had Arlene on his mind. That alone would be motivation to unpack the car quickly so that they could sit comfortably together and enjoy being together.

He reached the parking lot, opened the back door to throw his jacket in the back seat where he might find some room. He got in the front and had just adjusted himself. Ready to turn the key and he noticed an envelope under the windshield wiper on the driver's side.

He got out and looked at the handwriting. No doubt it was from Hannah. Now what?

Bevan Brothers

"Mrs. Stillings, could you get Donavon Bevan on the phone for me? He is up in Spencer. It will be under Bevan Electronics."

"No problem."

Noel had given Donavon time to think about starting his own store in Emerald. He threw out the proposition a week earlier. He was hoping Donavon would have called him but since that didn't happen, he was making the call. Just as well, he liked to keep on top of things.

"Bevan Electronics, Julius speaking, how can I help you?"

"Noel Dahlke calling for Donavon Bevan. Is he available?"

"Sure thing, hold on and I will get him for you." Julius called across the room. "Donavon, Noel is calling for you."

"Be right there." Donavon was putting together the latest in fine stereo equipment and was glad to take a break. It wasn't going as smoothly as he thought it would.

"Donovan on line 2 for you."

"Thanks Mrs. Stillings." Line 2 was pushed. "Donavon, how are things going up there in Spencer?"

"Hey, Noel, pretty good for the most part. How about you in Emerald?"

"Oh, things are booming down here. Great little town we got. The only thing missing is an electronics store by one of those Bevan brothers."

Donavon couldn't help but smile. He knew what kind of a salesman Noel could be. "Is that right? Well, I better get right on down there and take care of that!" He kidded.

"So you think it is in the cards for you to start up your own business in our community?"

"Well, Jules and I have been talking about it. And it probably won't be so much my own business as an expansion of OUR business."

"That works for me. Anything to get you down here. And I don't think you'll be disappointed. When are you coming down to take a look at us?"

"How does the end of the week work for you?"

"Perfect! Give me a call when you have a time set in place."

"Will do!"

The Letter

He debated whether to open it now or later. His curiosity got the best of him. He decided to open it now before he took off for Emerald. He also decided that the letter would stay in Iowa City. He wanted to make sure that Arlene never saw it.

It was heavily perfumed. He could tell that by merely holding it in his hands. And that bothered him a little as he didn't want Arlene to get a whiff of a different fragrance. A good washing of the hands would help.

Thankfully, the letter was only one page long. It was handwritten. She did have nice handwriting. He could say that for her. As he started to read it... well... he didn't know how he felt. It began like one of Arlene's letters: Dearest Brian.

He gave out a big sigh and thought, "Oh-oh." It didn't take long to read what Hannah wrote. But he had to read it two or three times to get the full impact.

While nothing specific was coming out in what she wrote, it still bothered him. He got the impression that she thought they had a special relationship, which, he guessed, they did, but not in the same way she was thinking.

She wrote that she hoped they would see each other over the summer. "Where did that come from?" he thought.

But the thing that bothered him the most was how she ended the letter. She drew a heart and then signed it "Love, Hannah."

Once again, Brian thought, "Oh-oh."

The Clinic

Ginger was headed out the door and on her way to meet with Anita for lunch. There was somewhat of a backup that was evidenced by a full waiting room. As often happens, when the doctor spends more time than expected with one patient, everyone else has to wait. And that can be irritating except for the fact that no one wants the doctor to rush through THEIR appointment.

The Clinic had enough help that Ginger could be gone for a while. After all, she was the head of the nurses, overseer, something like that.

As she was exiting, Shirley Nieting was about to enter, and Ginger held the door for her. "Hurt your foot, Shirley?" Ginger noticed she was dragging it somewhat.

"No, why do you ask?"

"Well, it appeared that you were kind of dragging it a little."

"Really? I didn't notice. Maybe that is the reason I have been having problems with my leg."

"That why you are here to see Dr. Floyd?"

"You never know. It might be all connected."

"Well, hope he figures it out for you."

"Me, too." And with a smile they both went their separate ways.

The Café

"Where is everyone?" Ginger asked as she entered the café.

"That is what I would like to know." Dorothy responded as she poured Ginger a cup of coffee, waiting for Anita to come over. "It has been pretty quiet all morning. There was the expected morning rush and then... nothing."

"You suppose there is mass dieting going on?" Ginger smiled.

Dorothy tilted her head and said, "Guess we'll see." Before she left she asked, "Is Anita coming over too?"

"Yeah, she'll be here in a minute."

And with that another cup was poured which turned out to be perfect timing as Anita just rounded the corner.

"So, how's your morning been going?"

"Can't complain. Since I do more managing than nursing, most days are pretty quiet."

"Does that bother you, I mean, not actually putting on band-aids, that kind of thing." Anita asked as she got comfortable in the booth.

"Mmm, sometimes. I do like being in on the action. But more and more, my position seems to include a lot of filing, paperwork, and PR, you know just talking with people."

"I think I know what you mean."

"Yeah, like this morning, as I left, Shirley Nieting was coming in. I talked with her for a while. She is so easy to talk to. You know what I mean?"

"I do. And since you brought her up, I have to ask you, did you notice a limp?"

Ginger said, "I did. I wonder if anything is wrong."

"Could be just arthritis."

"Probably is. Maybe she is having Dr. Floyd check it out."

On to another subject, Anita asked, "Did you get your invitation to Noel and Angela's wedding?"

"Yes, I did. Finally they are tying the knot."

"I know. About time. They make a good-looking couple." And

more chit-chat took place for the next hour or so.

Home at Last

Driving by the high school he felt kind of nostalgic. That building held a lot of memories from the last four years. He had been involved in various extracurricular activities and had been challenged in some of the classes he took. But the best memories were of his senior year and the relationship he had with Arlene.

The busses were just pulling up in front of school, one behind the other, waiting to be filled by scholars who had about had it with school. Only a couple weeks left, and they would enjoy their freedom.

Brian wondered what kind of freedom he would have this summer. He knew he had to find work somewhere. And there were various places he could apply for summer work. He already had some in mind. But as far as he was concerned, there was no rush.

His thoughts were solely on getting his car unpacked, everything put away for the summer and then seeing Arlene. He assumed she was working at the store. He didn't know if he would see her today or have to wait until tomorrow. Well, he could at least drive through downtown.

He often wondered what her day was like. What was her routine? How did she approach each day? He knew that not a day went by that he wasn't thinking of her. Was she thinking about him?

Parked on the street he started to unpack his vehicle. It took several trips and his room that was clean and tidy now looked anything but! Ah, he had the whole summer to put things away. No big rush.

It was a little before five that he decided to call Hakeman's and see if Arlene was available.

"Hakeman's Cards and Things, how can I help you?"

Believe it or not, for the first time ever, at least as far as he was concerned, Arlene answered the phone. He thought he would have some fun with her. "Uh, is that a trick question or something. I mean, I think you can help me in a lot of ways. Where do I begin?"

"Brian, you're home!"

"Well, for at least the next three months, maybe longer." He smiled as he was glad to hear her excited voice. "Want to go to Pop's tonight?"

"Do I? When can you pick me up?"

"When do you get off?"

"Uh, in about 65 minutes." And then she continued, "But if you want to come early, that would be okay. I am the only one in the store right now. In fact I will be closing."

Brian got a big grin on his face. "See you in five minutes!" And he was out the door.

The Summer Begins

Five minutes passed and then ten minutes. When ten stretched into fifteen, Arlene wondered where in the world Brian could be. What was taking him so long.

She had already made sure she was looking her best. A crisp floral blouse and bright skirt, though not too bright was what he would see. Hair was just perfect, and she brought along the perfume that drove him crazy, at least that is what he said. A little sprayed here and a little there. And maybe a “do I dare” spray there.

Finally he pulls up and parks right in front of the store. Not a lot of traffic this time of day. He gets out of the car, and she watches him every step of the way but doesn’t go to greet him as he comes in. She wants him to see her from afar. Hopefully he will get more excited with every step he takes. She knows she will.

“Hey there!” Brian is smiling from ear to ear.

“What took you so long?” She teases.

“Well, to be honest, when I called you I had just finished unpacking my car. Didn’t smell too good. Couldn’t come and see my Babe smelling like that. Had to take a shower.”

“So, I’m your Babe, huh?” She teased him with a provocative look and eyebrows raised.

"You bet you are," and he took her in his arms and gave her a long overdue kiss.

No one was in the store to witness this public display of affection. But just to make sure, Arlene led him to the back area where they could get in one more long kiss.

Finally, they cooled it for a while knowing more would come later.

"So, where is the boss lady?"

"Oh, Angela and Noel had some wedding stuff to take care of in Alcoa and she took off early."

"And she left you with taking care of the whole place by yourself?"

"Yeah. Why? Don't you think I can handle it?"

"Oh, no, nothing like that. I was just wondering how many guys you might attract, you being here by yourself."

"The answer is NONE. Everyone knows I'm taken."

They loved teasing one another like that. They talked about all kinds of things, never taking their eyes off one another.

"Well, we going to Pop's tonight?" Arlene asked as she was putting the cash away in the safe.

"Sounds good."

Lights were turned off and the door was locked.

Pop's

They had to drive around for a little while. And the only reason for that was so that he could have his arm around her, and they could feel the closeness of the other. It had been far too long. And the drive was a slow one.

They took the back way to Jewel Lake and sped up a little only when a car was behind them. Otherwise it was a very lazy drive. The sun wasn't going down too soon and so they walked down to the lake at the State Park. Walking hand in hand never got old.

Finally seated at Pop's, a more serious conversation began.

"I've been thinking about applying for summer work at Fitgerald's first and see if they need anyone. If that doesn't pan out, I will see if Emerald Hydraulics is looking for any help."

Arlene took a sip of her drink. "I would think that between the two you would be able to find some work."

"I would too. But you never know. If I have to, I will see if any farmers need help. There is always walking beans or stacking hay bales." Brian said. "I kind of enjoyed that but it doesn't pay that much."

Arlene asked, "Have you decided if you are going back to Iowa

City or not?"

Brian looked to the side. "As far as I am concerned, I am definitely NOT going back to Iowa City. But I haven't told my parents yet."

"What do you think they will say?"

"That's just it. I don't know. They may not say anything. Or..."

"Or?"

"Or... they might ask why I am making that decision."

"Yeah," Arlene said, "because of me?"

"That is what they will assume."

They were both quiet for a while.

Arlene made an iffy face and asked, "Is that bad?"

"Not as far as I'm concerned. I mean, they know I gave you a Promise Ring. They know what that means." He looked at her and asked, "Why? Are you having second thoughts?"

"NEVER!" Arlene made the statement in an almost emphatic way and then got a little embarrassed.

An Unexpected Confession

Brian thought he would ask Arlene about her plans. "So, are you going to work for Angela or Michael? What are your plans?"

"I don't know. With Angela getting married in June, I know that she would really like me to help Shirley take care of the store while they are on their honeymoon." Then Arlene put her hand out saying, "On the other hand, I would kind of like to get more experience with Michael. I just don't know."

"Arlene, I've got something to confess."

"You do?"

"Yeah."

"Is it bad?"

Brian was quick to reassure her it wasn't bad. "No nothing like that. At least I am not looking at it as being bad. It has to do with us, with you and me and our future."

"Okay, what is it?"

"I've been doing a lot of thinking..."

"And?"

"And..." he took a deep breath, "you seem to have all kinds of thoughts about what you would like to do with your life and are so positive on photography. And I get the feeling that if that didn't work, you would work in Hakeman's or someplace like that, maybe get your own store. I don't know."

"Okay."

Brian kind of shook his head. "This last year at Iowa City, well, I got a taste of college, and it was okay, but I guess I don't have the dreams you have or the same feeling about journalism that I once had."

"Okay. What does that mean? What are you saying. And even more important, what does that have to do with us?" Arlene looked straight at Brian.

Brian put his hand up to his face. His eyes went back and forth. Finally he said, "Arlene, I've been wondering, what if I didn't go back to college? What if I found a job here in Emerald? Not just a summer job but a full-time job. What would you think?"

"What do you mean, what would I think?"

"I mean, would you be disappointed in me? Would your thoughts about me change? Would you still want to be with me?"

She got a worried look on her face and with a questioning expression asked, "Why would I? What you do in life ... I love you for you, not your job or anything like that." Then she asked, "Are you really thinking along those lines?"

A Call From Mom

Mother's Day over, the theme for the store took on an Emerald Days focus. Angela always had various items that took people back to 1986 and the tornado that changed everything. Eventually Father's Day and the Fourth of July would slowly creep out of the backroom as well.

Shirley wasn't feeling so well and so Arlene picked up the slack. And Arlene made the decision that Hakeman's was where she wanted to work. Michael understood and left the offer on the table should Arlene ever desire to work there... she could.

"Glad you could spend the day with me as Shirley asked for time off." Angela smiled as Arlene brought a box out of the back.

Arlene gave a look that revealed she was happy to be there. "Well, I'm glad it all worked out." She put the box on the counter.

"You really liked working with Michael?"

"I did." Before she went on she added, "But I also like working here. And I don't mind the extra hours."

"Well, I am glad you do. Have you given any more thought to putting in more hours, working while Noel and I are on our honeymoon?"

Before Arlene could answer the phone rang.

"Well think about that while I get the phone. Hakeman's Card's and Things, this is Angela, how can I help you."

"Angela, this is Mom. How are you?"

"Mom! Good to hear from you." And then as always she asked, "Is everything okay? Dad fine?"

"Oh, yes, everybody up here is doing okay. Just called... well I called for a couple of reasons."

"Okay."

"All the wedding plans getting taken care of? Everything on schedule?"

"Well, I think so. Sent out the invitations and have gotten a good number of responses already."

"That sounds good."

"And I had the final fitting for my dress this last weekend."

"Oh, I can hardly wait to see it. I am sure you will look beautiful."

"Well, it cost enough!"

And then there was silence for a moment.

"Angela, I have a question for you."

"Okay."

Her mother hesitated for a moment. "Uh, I don't mean to pry but are you and your brother getting along now?"

Angela looked at the phone as if something was wrong with it. "Why do you ask?"

"Well... Glenn called me the other day and said ..."

"Said what?"

"He said he got an invitation to your wedding." There was silence on the line. "I just thought maybe you, uh... reconciled.

Angela didn't know what to say.

Dr. Floyd

She felt old sitting in the uncomfortable chair. The padding wasn't so good any longer. It was the only one left. It was a busy day in The Clinic. Two nurses were behind the counter checking people in. A third nurse had just taken back a mother and her three-year-old.

Ginger Kemp appeared and disappeared on a regular basis keeping everything organized and under control. She took a minute to look up and she saw Shirley sitting in that one chair that should have been thrown away a long time ago.

Ginger came around the counter. "Good morning Shirley. How are we doing today?"

"Well, right now I am doing pretty good, but my weekend wasn't so... well, it could have been better."

"You have an appointment with Dr. Floyd?"

"Yes, he said he thought he could squeeze me in if I came right away." Then she corrected herself. "Well, he didn't say that but one of the nurses did. And so, here I am." She said it with a smile on her face.

And no sooner had she said it than the nurse at the counter called her name. Shirley got up and went to the mystery area behind the counter to find out what was going on in her body.

When the doctor came into the room, Shirley had the opportunity to share what had been going on with her. After a brief examination Dr. Floyd shared his thoughts.

"Shirley, over the past few months we have seen a change in your walking basically but also in your balance and other things."

"What do you think is wrong doctor?"

"Well, it could be a number of things, but I am really not sure."

"Okay."

"I would like to refer you to a specialist in Alcoa."

"A specialist?"

"Yes. You see it could be nothing or it could be serious. I don't want to upset you or tell you anything more. And I would have to say that I really don't think it is serious. But the specialist will be able to give a better diagnosis."

"Well, if you think it is best."

"I do."

Dr. Floyd gave her the name and number of the next doctor she would see.

Eventide

December 1

So much had taken place over the last year. A lot of changes were seen. And change can be good, but it can also be unsettling. You plan and imagine in your mind how your future will be shaped. You see it clearly. But how do you get from point A to point B. And maybe it isn't point B that you are aiming for. Maybe it is point G or even point T. Life can get complicated.

Brian was getting dressed for church. His family had already left, and he was alone in the house. He wouldn't be meeting them. They would be in a different building altogether. He would be attending worship with Arlene. This was going to be a first. And he was just a little nervous.

Seeing the two of them sitting together in church as the Advent/Christmas season began, well, a lot of tongues would be wagging and in the minds of many their future was already decided.

In his mind he thought it also had been decided. It seemed like it had been years ago that he gave Arlene the Promise Ring when it had only been last spring. How excited they both were when the ring was placed on her finger. When he gave it to her he had no idea how long it would be before he might purchase another ring. Would it be months? Would it be years? After all, he had three more years of college. Or did he?

The December morning has a nip to it. It is not unbelievably cold, but you do need a coat. He pulls up to her house. She is the only one home. Her parents are already at church. He doesn't have to ring the doorbell. She is watching for him. No dress today. A pair of dress slacks and a sweater make her look beautiful. She wears heels that give a little more height.

"You look gorgeous."

"You look pretty handsome yourself." She smiles and flirts a little. As he helps her with her coat she asks, "Are you ready for this? You know there will be a number of ladies taking notice."

"I suppose so. I am not worried about them. I am worried about all the guys who will see you."

Arlene smiled and said, "Ah, but you see, they will know I have been... well, you know."

Just a slight peck of a kiss along with a hug and they were off. Didn't want to mess up the lipstick.

Looking For Work

He had high hopes. Finding summer employment was not supposed to be all that difficult. But so far he had struck out everywhere he went.

Fitzgerald Manufacturing has already hired some high school students and they seemed to be working out fine. Right now everything was looking good, and they weren't planning on hiring any more workers unless they got in a pinch. They would keep Brian's application on file.

No problem. Emerald Hydraulics was a great supporter of college students looking for a place to work, spend some time, earn some money. Brian went to the personnel office, filled out everything he needed to and was told he would get a call when they started to need summer help. So far, no call.

He applied at the new coffee and ice cream place in town, but they weren't hiring. He hoped that when the stereo place opened, maybe they would need someone but heard that was doubtful.

"So, what are you going to do?" Jared had just heard the dismal report on Brian's attempt to find work.

Brian wasn't in too good a mood, "Well, I don't know. Didn't think it would be this difficult. I do have a job on Friday baling hay. Guess I could do a lot of farm stuff this summer."

Arlene asked, "I didn't think you liked doing that."

"I don't necessarily but it beats sitting around." He gave her a look that revealed how down he felt.

Brenda added, "Wish we needed someone at the store, but we are at a pretty good point where we are at." Then she looked at Jared, "Don't you think?"

Brian didn't give up on continuing to look for employment. But for the time being, nothing seemed to be available.

What Next?

She wasn't sure what was going to happen next. Her wedding was just a few weeks off and it seemed that problem after problem was surfacing.

The biggest problem of all was that her estranged brother got an invitation by mistake... kind of. Angela's mom sent a list of people she thought should be at the wedding. Included in that list was Angela's brother. In addressing invitations on that afternoon,

Noel just assumed every name sent by Angela's mom would be okay. And Angela felt the same. Little did she know what her mom had cooked up. Bottom line, her brother Glenn was coming.

And then the whole situation with Shirley. Shirley had been working for Angela for years. It worked out perfectly. Angela was looking for help. Shirley had the time, and the extra cash would help out the family. She was a good employee. Very dependable. Very mature. And then, as of late, she had been having problems. She wasn't old enough to have "old people" problems.

And finally, God bless her, Arlene had become a fixture at Hakeman's. She surpassed all Angela's expectation of what an employee so young would be like. Conscientious. Courteous. Prompt. Efficient. She couldn't say enough good things about her. But... would she be staying or not? Would she start her own business? She didn't know what was going on for sure in her mind.

Everything seemed to be up in the air.

Arlene and Brian

"Have you talked to your parents yet?" Arlene was asking the question. Brian avoided looking at her. Something hard for him to do. Usually he was always looking into her eyes.

"Not really. And I don't know when the right time will be." They were talking about his plans for the future. "And maybe I want to be sure about what I am doing before I talk to them."

"Make sure about what? You and me?"

"No, I didn't mean it that way. I meant about taking classes at the junior college, that kind of thing."

"Do you think they will object to you NOT going back to Iowa City?"

"I don't think so. I mean, I think I kind of pushed that on them, insisting it was the best place for me to get what I was looking for in journalism."

They sat there in silence for a while.

Brian brought up work again. "Anyway, I have to find a job for the summer somewhere. I have got a lot on my mind."

Arlene stretched out to hold his hand. "I hope I am on your mind."

He looked up at her and smiled. "Always."

Arlene took a deep breath and then unexpectedly asked, "Have you ever thought about working at Hakeman's?"

"You mean where you work? Your Hakeman's?"

"Do you know another?"

"What would I do?"

"The same thing I do!"

"Is Angela looking for more help? How much does she pay?"

"I would have to answer, 'I don't know' to all your questions. I just thought that maybe with Shirley cutting back a little, Angela might need some help."

Brian thought for a bit. "I don't know if I could work at the same place you do."

"Why?"

"Do I have to explain it?"

And then the light bulb came on over Arlene's head. "Oh! I don't know. Then again Jared and Brenda work at the same place."

"But that is different."

Davenport

The summer was killing her. She didn't have a job although she could probably get one part-time... somewhere. But she really wasn't that excited about getting a job. She spent some time hanging around with girlfriends from high school. But most of them had their own lives, own jobs, own boyfriends, and that made her even more depressed.

She was hoping her old boyfriend would call and ... she didn't know what. And then she wondered if any other guys might call. She didn't know if news about their breakup got around or not. If they were still in high school, it would have spread like wildfire. But now that they were out of the circle, it might be something different.

At any rate, no one had called. And this led her to thinking about her first year at college. And maybe it would be her only year. After all, she was just following her boyfriend, basically. She had no big plans on taking on a career.

But there was also something else that popped up when she thought about her time in Iowa City. His name was Brian. She had begun to get close to him. Was it purely one sided? She didn't know. He gave no indications he was interested in her. And he did have a girlfriend back in ... where did he live again? He mentioned it once or twice.

Hannah was wondering what to do. Brian helped her out with her Kevin problems in the past. Maybe he could help now. Or would that look too obvious? Where did he live? She was trying to remember. North central Iowa. It started with an "E". Estherville? No. Emmetsburg? No, that didn't sound right. She tapped her lips trying to figure out what the name of the town might be. Nothing came to mind. She would have to give it more thought.

Memorial Day

Well, it was kind of a social event. It was something the whole town attended: The Memorial Day Observance in the public cemetery. It was a quiet Monday morning. None of the businesses were open, except Bonnie's Café. They would close before noon.

Downtown had a smattering of cars. Most of them, well, all of them actually, belonged to the local Amvets members. They were all in dress uniforms. Older guys who had to order uniforms a little larger than when they were in the service.

Over at the school students are doing what they need to do to provide the patriotic music everyone was waiting to hear. Soon they will be lining up to march downtown and then the cemetery.

Loved ones spent the previous day decorating graves of loved ones. Only the really older graves seem to lack color.

This is what one might call a spring homecoming. Students who have been away at college are eager to see old classmates who are almost sure to be here.

By 9:00 this Monday morning, more activity is happening. Cars find a spot to park off to the side of the road in the cemetery.

Kids are running around, and people are gathering in groups talking about the weather, the crops, and what they are doing later.

Brian parks at the first available space. He gets out and Arlene follows him. Both are dressed for the summer. Both are wearing shorts. Brian has a blue polo shirt on, and Arlene wears a pullover blouse that Brian can't get enough of. Hand in hand they slowly drift toward where the ceremony takes place.

"Look at those white legs!" Jared points to Brian's legs begging for a tan. Brian can't respond as Jared is wearing jeans.

Brian looks down and tries to think of a comeback. But he is a blank. Still he says, "Yeah, well, you just wait..."

Before he can finish Jared smiles and says, "Ouch, that really stung," mocking Brian's lack of response.

Arlene's legs already have a bit of a tan and Brian wishes he had more of one. A change of subject is in order.

"You all ready for the picnic?" The two couples will be together out at Jewel Lake where they have a special place they will be together. The girls have figured out the menu. Too cold to swim, they are all looking forward to a relaxing and possibly romantic time?

Memorial Day—Another Perspective

"Morning Ange!" Noel walks right on in. The front door is open, and he lets the screen door slam.

Angela is in the kitchen cleaning up after breakfast. From behind it looks like she is wearing shorts but as she turns it looks like a miniskirt.

"Wow, Ms. Hakeman do you look foxy or what?" Noel has a great big smile on his face.

She turns toward him and does an eyebrow thing that shows she appreciates the compliment. This is only moments before he has his arms around her, and an early morning kiss is enjoyed. And that is followed with a pat on her behind.

"You about ready to go?" Noel asks as he stretches a little.

"I think so." And then she adds, "Do you feel like walking?"

"I don't know. Do you?"

"Yeah, why not? It is so nice out."

They are not alone. Parking would be at a premium at the cemetery and since the temperature was just right and the sun was shining, it was a good call.

Hand in hand with sunglasses well in place they take off.

"Can you believe that it is only a few short weeks before we will be married?" Noel brings it up.

Angela looks at him and asks, "You getting nervous?"

"Not in the least," he smiles back. "Can't wait!"

"Me either." Then Angela remembered, "That reminds me, did you make the reservations for the rehearsal dinner?"

"Long time ago, Ange. Remember you are marrying a man who pays attention to detail."

"Yeah, well we'll see as time goes on," she kidded.

"Hey you two." They were interrupted by Jeff and Anita as they were also on the trek to the cemetery. "It won't be long now."

"We were just talking about that," Angela shared, and the couples walked the rest of the way together. Anita and Angela held up most of the conversation.

All this talk about the wedding was fine but Angela still had that pit in her stomach, wondering if her brother would show up or not. "He wouldn't, would he?"

An Unwanted Diagnosis

Shirley was hearing the news for the first time and taking it surprisingly well, considering the circumstances. Actually, she wondered if it was accurate or not. She felt fine. She hadn't had any ... any of the problems she had earlier. Maybe the diagnosis was wrong.

The doctor looked at her and said, "I'm sorry. The test was conclusive. I'm afraid there is no doubt. You have multiple sclerosis, MS."

"But I feel fine now."

"And you may feel that way for the rest of your life. You never know. Or you might show some of the symptoms on occasion. It is too early to tell."

"Well," Shirley asked, "what do I do now? Is there medicine I can take? Or, just what do I need to do?"

The doctor gave her all kinds of information about MS that she could take home and read. He also told her of the latest breakthroughs in curbing the symptoms. It was all a little overwhelming at the time as one would expect.

Shirley was a reader, and she got all the information she could regarding symptoms and ways of treating MS. When she got to work the next day she told Angela what was happening. And even though she showed no signs of MS, what could possibly happen.

Angela listened and sympathized with her. Personally, Angela didn't know anyone who had MS and so it was all new to her. When Arlene came in, she also got filled in on what was happening.

No one seemed to be worried too much about Shirley's condition since she wasn't really showing any signs that something was wrong.

"I don't mean to sound uncaring, but do you think that you will still be able to handle things when I am on my honeymoon?"

Shirley looked around and said, "I don't see why not! I feel like I always have. All those symptoms that took me to the doctor, haven't felt them for a while now. I say it is a go!"

But before the week was out, no one was sure about it or not.

Thursday

When Shirley told everyone about the diagnosis, she thought it was all a lot of excitement about nothing. She felt good. She was walking okay and none of the things she read about MS, and she read a lot, were happening to her. But that was not to last long.

Wednesday she felt fine. She went to work like always. At noon she went home and took care of all her chores just like always. Thursday morning she got ready for work. Made some cinnamon rolls to take for everyone to snack on. Once again, everything seemed fine.

It was a busy morning. Emerald Days was fast approaching. Had to get a lot ready. It was getting close to noon and about time for Arlene to show up. Shirley had just replenished some greeting cards and was on her way back to the counter, Arlene just entered, and as Shirley slightly turned around, she fell to the floor, taking a display down with her!

Her fall brought Angela out of the backroom and Arlene also rushed to help her up.

Angela said, “Are you alright? Are you hurt?”

“Let me help you.” Arlene was there to help also.

“Oh, I am so clumsy. Don’t know what happened.” As she tried to get up she couldn’t move her legs.

“What’s wrong?” Angela asked as Shirley wasn’t using her legs to get up.

“I don’t know! I just can’t get up. My legs won’t move.”

“Arlene, call 9-1-1.”

The call was made, and Dr. Floyd also arrived. MS was rearing its ugly head.

What To Do Now?

Shirley was out of commission, at least for now. Dr. Floyd said that it was common in some MS patients, such … things will come and go. Tomorrow she could feel fine. But Friday she didn't feel fine. Who knew what the future held in store.

Angela felt bad for Shirley but the business side of her was getting jittery. She needed to find more help for Arlene. She was going to be short-handed BIG TIME.

There were some part-time workers she could call on, but they were not a sure thing. Arlene was called in to work more hours than usual and she didn't mind. She could help out. Still, more help was needed.

"Angela, could I talk with you for a minute?"

"Sure, what's up?"

"I've been thinking about this for a while now and … I don't know, I feel kind of funny asking or even mentioning it."

Angela smiled at her, "Just spit it out."

"Okay. Okay. Well as we will be shorthanded for a while and maybe for quite a while and with your wedding coming up..."

"What do you want to say Arlene?"

"Well, I was wondering, Brian is looking for a job. Would you consider hiring him to fill in while Shirley is out?"

"Brian? Your Brian? Do you think he would like working here?" Then Angela said, "That's a stupid question. Of course he wouldn't mind working here. As long as you are here."

Arlene blushed a little. "I think he would be a great asset. And not just because he is my boyfriend. He has got a way about him that... well... I think he would be perfect."

"You do, huh?" Angela gave a little bit of a smirk.

Arlene put her finger to her lips and thought about what she would say next. "I tell you what, Angela. With your permission let me talk to him, ask him how he feels and then if he is interested, I'll ask him to come in for an interview. That okay?"

Of course it was. And later that same day, Brian, in shirt and tie was sitting in the back room with Angela, looking like the salesman of the year.

Hakeman's

With both Arlene and Brian, for now, working for Angela, it didn't go without notice that there seemed to be a coordination with what they were wearing. That meant that whatever Arlene was wearing on a certain day, Brian's shirt and/or tie seemed to match perfectly. Of course Arlene picked everything out. And in some cases they had to go to Richards Clothing to find new things for Brian to wear.

And any concern that Angela had about his working there was dismissed. Yeah, you could tell that these two people were love-birds, but they gave a feeling of concern for every customer and worked very well together.

And as Angela's wedding day grew closer and closer, she felt better about leaving it all in the hands of Arlene and Brian. She felt confident that they could handle it all. She was only going to be gone for a week.

Angela didn't know if having a guy working in the store would be a good thing or not. But she found out that as Arlene brought in some of the male clientele, so also Brian did the same with some of the females. Yes, most knew about the Brian and Arlene thing but still.

Wedding Day Fears and Apprehensions

Taking care of the store was one thing. Calming her nerves regarding her wedding was another. For the most part everything seemed to fall in place perfectly, or close to it.

The schedule was followed. She knew when people would arrive. Reservations were confirmed. The photographer, who just happened to be Michael Stepchild and her assistant Arlene Plummer, were ready and waiting. A million things to take care of and 999,999 had fallen right in line.

Only one thing was still bugging her: her brother. He got an invitation. Would he actually come? Would he have the nerve? Maybe he thought she had a change of heart, which she didn't. And if he came would it ruin everything? At first she felt it would. And she felt that way for the longest time.

But she decided that with all the hurt he had caused in the past, she was not going to allow him to give her anxiety now. If he did come, she knew if she asked, her parents would run interference, and keep him at bay, if necessary. But she also felt that she was going to be above it all. She was going to show him she didn't care one way or the other. At least she felt she could pull that off.

Eventide

Arlene and Brenda

A pretty young brunette is sitting at a table in Bonnie's Café. She is dressed professionally. She has perfect posture and catches the eye of many a young man. Holding a cup of tea with both hands and sipping occasionally, she waits for her best friend to join her. She is deep in thought.

Finally, her friend arrives. Not dressed even close to the fashion her friend is, she notices how nice she looks. But each has their own job requiring different attire.

Christmas music is faintly playing in the background as Brenda joins Arlene for a midmorning break.

"So, what's up?" Brenda sits down next to Arlene in case the conversation is going to get extra personal.

Arlene looks over her cup. "Oh, I just wanted to talk, you know, just you and me, without the guys."

"Sounds mysterious. What did you want to talk about?"

Arlene puts her cup down, looks away for a second and then said, "It is about me and Brian."

"Of course it is. What is going on now?"

Arlene played with her Promise Ring. "Brenda, I have to ask you something."

"Okay..."

"Have a... have you and Jared... uh... ever thought about eloping?"

Brenda put her hand up to her mouth and with eyes as big as they could be. "You and Brian are going to elope? Really!"

"I didn't say that. I just asked if you and Jared ever considered that."

Brenda calmed down and said, "No. Why would we ever do that?"

" I don't know... just asking."

Eventide

Arlene and Brenda, Part 2

Brenda wasn't sure where all this was going and was really surprised that Arlene brought up the subject of eloping at all. She had to find out more.

"Jared and I will be getting married. I know that for sure. And I also know that I want a big church wedding. I want the bridesmaids, I want the dress, I want the reception. I want it all. Don't you?"

Arlene gave Brenda a look that affirmed what Brenda thought. "Of course I do. I want all the things you want."

"Then why the eloping thing?"

"Because I don't know if our parents will go for that, I mean, as soon as we would want to get married."

"How soon are you thinking?"

"Well, I think Brian is going to give me a ring for Christmas."

"Really?"

"Yeah. He has been saving up his money, has become the little miser, and if he does propose, well, I don't think he will want a long engagement."

"Forget about him, do YOU want a long engagement?"

"Not really and that means sometime next year we would, you know, get married."

Brenda sat up straight and tried to organize all Arlene's thoughts. "Okay, so you think Brian is going to propose and you, of course, would accept. But you don't think your parents, or his parents will go for it?"

"That's it."

"Well, have you asked them?"

Coffee, Cakes, and Cream

Mike McCarty couldn't be happier. The store he had to close down because competition drove him out of business, had now been reopened in a different location and was going gangbusters.

And one of the good aspects about it was that it was not ruining anyone else's business and filling a need the town of Emerald didn't even know it had.

It was a dream come true and from day one it was accepted as part of the Emerald business district. It was up and running the middle of May and just in time for the closing of a school year and not too far after that, Emerald Days. It was the perfect place for parents to take their children for special days, like birthdays and for ordinary days, just for a treat.

And finding people to work was not a problem either. During the summer he had all the help he needed. This move to Emerald was just what his store needed.

Douglas Hardware enjoyed that move as well. First of all, the lease was cut in half, lowering overhead. But second, pedestrian traffic did increase on East Main and more sales were being made.

The New Employee

If Angela had any doubts about whether to hire Brian as part-time help when Shirley was having her problems, those doubts went out the window as soon as he put in his first week.

Arlene was in charge of training him and she took it seriously. His demeanor in the store, his appearance, the way he helped customers while not being pushy, she taught him everything.

And wanting to do the best job possible, he took what Arlene said as Gospel. While nervous at first, he got the hang of it very quickly. And he started to enjoy it.

Working with Arlene could be a distraction, but he worked on just being a good employee. When no one was around, well, they did find times, down times, to talk. But most of the talk was store talk, not relationship talk.

One more thing Angela noticed as did Arlene. They looked at it differently, however.

When Arlene started her time at Hakeman's, the number of young men who shopped there increased. Well, maybe they didn't always purchase something, but they spent time in the store. Would Brian draw a response from... young ladies?

The answer to that question is a resounding YES! Oh, it didn't happen immediately, but getting closer to Noel and Angela's wedding, it appeared that some younger girls, basically freshmen and sophomores would browse through the aisles.

Arlene noticed it and thought to herself how young they were and how obvious they were. This led her to wonder if she appeared the same way at times. Was she ever that young? Was she ever that immature? She didn't dwell on it. And it didn't bother her that these young girls found Brian attractive. They definitely weren't competition.

But she saw someone else as competition. And she didn't know what to make of her.

Where Did She Come From?

The Saturday afternoon, one week before the wedding, Hakeman's became swamped for some reason. The store had more customers than it usually did on the weekend. And everyone was busy helping wherever they could.

The crowd was made up mostly of women in their twenties and thirties. There were a few teenagers of both genders. Angela was at the counter and Arlene and Brian were moving around in various areas.

Arlene had just found the box for a figurine a customer was sending to a relative. As Arlene turned around to see if anyone else needed help she witnessed something strange. Brian was hugging a young lady and even though he wasn't holding her tight, she seemed to have him in a bear hug, not wanting to let him go.

Needless to say, Arlene wondered what was going on. Brian didn't look embarrassed by what happened until... until he saw Arlene watching the activity. He knew he had to clear this up. He did so by bringing the young woman over to Arlene.

"Arlene, this is Hannah Carpenter. Hannah, this is my girlfriend, Arlene." Then turning to Arlene and intentionally getting closer to her he continued, looking at Arlene, "Remember, I told you about Hannah who went to school in Iowa City."

Arlene displayed a puzzled look.

Brian was trying to give hints about who Hannah was. "She helped me in finding stationary... I helped her with some of her, uh, problems and she..."

Fortunately, he didn't have to go further. Arlene remembered the note she found. "Oh, yes, I remember you mentioning Hannah." Then she turned to welcome Hannah even more while at the same time taking Brian's hand. And that didn't go without notice by Hannah either.

Arlene smiled as she asked, "So what are you doing here in Emerald?"

"Well, I am on my way up to Okoboji. I'm going to work at a church camp up there for a couple weeks. And when I saw the sign that directed me to Emerald, I decided to check it out and see if Brian was here. Went to the café and asked if by chance Brian Seagren was around and lo and behold, they pointed me in this direction and... here I am."

A moment of silence happened after Hannah shared so much. And then looking at Arlene she said, "Arlene, I have heard so much about you. And you are just as pretty as Brian described you. Maybe a little more."

Arlene was beginning to feel better about this meeting.

And then Hannah put her hands on both of Brian's shoulders and said, "Guess what? Kevin and I are back together!"

Pop's

"And when I turned around I saw this woman tightly embraced with my boyfriend! I thought they were going to start making out in the card section." Arlene was sharing with Jared and Brenda the excitement of Saturday afternoon at Hakeman's.

Brian knew she was only kidding. But in the back of his mind he couldn't help but remember that Hannah, poor rejected Hannah, had signed the note she placed on his car window, LOVE, Hannah. It was that note that didn't even get close to making it to Emerald.

He didn't want Arlene to see it and worry. And he had no qualms about disposing of it before he left Iowa City.

Brenda leans in to ask Arlene, "So was she cute?"

Arlene sips on her straw and kind of scrunches her face a little, "Uh, not so much. Nothing to worry about."

"And you have nothing to worry about anyway. You are still wearing that ring I gave you, aren't you?"

Arlene held out the ring and looked at it. "Yes, I am wearing it... until I get one to replace it." She smiled and raised her eyebrows. And then she said, "She thinks you are going back to Iowa City, doesn't she?"

"I guess she does. Didn't find an occasion to tell her. Shows how much I DON'T think about her."

"Good response," Arlene said.

What no one knew was that there was another female in Hakeman's that same day who noticed Brian and she would have quite an impact on Brian and Arlene.

Wedding Week

Angela was in the store off and on beginning on Monday of the week she and Noel would get married. She was there physically but not a whole lot mentally or emotionally. She had a lot on her mind.

Her parents would arrive on Wednesday. At least that was the plan. They would stay at her place and would leave for Young America sometime in the week that followed. Angela's place was getting a little crowded. Noel had been slowly bringing his stuff over and for now it was just being stacked wherever he could find room.

If they planned it right, he would be completely moved out of his place when his lease ended for the month. Their plan was to live at Angela's and do improvements on her place, make it what they wanted it to be.

But there was an aching feeling in Angela's mind. And it concerned her brother. Would he show up? Would he come? Why would he? He knows he is not wanted as far as I'm concerned? Would Mom egg him on and suggest he come? She just might!

Glenn hadn't sent an RSVP back. That in itself was a comfort. But it wasn't a guarantee. She knew him all too well. He was a master of deceit in the past. He would say one thing and do another. She tried to put him out of her mind. And on occasion it worked. It was only in weak moments where she should be daydreaming about her honeymoon and new life with Noel, that Glenn slowly crept in. She didn't fear him as she had in the past. But still...

Richards Clothing

Patrick and Tracy Richards had owned Richards Clothing since before the 1986 tornado. At that time they were only holding on to it by a thread, no pun intended. They didn't have the inventory they needed and hence, they didn't have the clientele either.

And the tornado took out their store completely. For a while they considered just taking the insurance and getting out of the business. But between Fred Kemp and Noel Dahlke they started to consider a new start. It might be risky. That was the way most business owners looked at it. Was the tornado a blessing in that insurance would help people who were struggling to move in a different direction?

Well, the tornado was a blessing in a way. And Patrick and Tracy found themselves on the positive side of what had happened. Shortly after the tornado went through Patrick's mother died and his father, Delbert, decided to sell the farm and if Patrick was interested, he, Delbert, would invest in the NEW Richards Clothing.

That was the motivating aspect in building the new store. The investment enabled them to expand their inventory in clothing for men and women.

And Delbert helped in another way. He became a full-time employee of Richards Clothing, in the Men's department. He was kind of a draw. He knew how to get sweaty and greasy working on the farm. But he also cleaned up pretty well to work in the store. He also had the gift to gab. He smiled a lot. All in all he was good at business.

But that was close to ten years ago. And his vitality wasn't what it was like back then. And full-time was in name only. His physical shape was wearing down, even though his attitude stayed the same.

Both Patrick and Tracy could see it and they knew something would have to change in the near future.

Wedding Week—Part Two

"When are your parents getting in?" Arlene asked.

Angela looked up at the ceiling as if the answer was there. "Well, early this afternoon, I think." And then she added, "That reminds me, I have to get Dad's tux from Richards. Maybe I can have Noel pick it up when he gets his."

Angela had a list. She always had a list, and she was crossing things off here and there when they were taken care of. She took a deep breath. "You're sure you and Brian can take care of things next week?"

"Oh," Arlene acted like it was a ridiculous question, "of course we can. Piece of cake. And if for some unknown reason we have a problem, Shirley is only a phone call away." She looked at Angela and said, "You have trained me so well, there are times I think I could take care of this place on my own... maybe."

Brian came up with merchandise a customer had picked out. "Just to let you know, we are out of these frames. This is the last one."

"I think we have another box in the back," Arlene was the first to respond, "Let me check."

After Brian finished with the customer, Angela asked him, "You and Arlene make a pretty good team, do you like working retail?"

"Yeah, I do." Brian responded. "Oh, working with Arlene, well, maybe I would like working wherever she was working. But, even if she wasn't working here, I think I would still enjoy it. Kind of surprises me a little." And then he asked, "Why do you ask? Am I doing something wrong?"

"Oh, nothing like that," she assured him, "just curious. You seem to have a knack with working with customers."

Arlene came back carrying a box of frames. "This is the last box. We better order more. It is one of themost popular items."

Angela smiled and saluted her, "Yes ma'am. I'll get right on it."

And at that moment, her parents arrived.

Richards Clothing

Marvin turned this way and then turned that way, looking at himself in the three-panel mirror.

Delbert stated, "For an old coot, you don't look half bad."

"I guess that is from one old coot to another." Marvin smiled.

"I guess it is." Delbert patted him on the back. "You getting excited about the wedding?"

"Oh, I suppose. Going to be a bigger affair than I ever imagined. I almost feel like a spectator. Noel's family is a lot larger than ours."

"Yeah, I guess it is."

Marvin went on. "I am really happy for Angela. I think they will make a great couple."

"Even give you some grandkids?"

Marvin turned his head a little and said, "You never know." He smiled back.

Delbert was sitting on a stool and as he got up, he acted like it was not so easy.

"You okay, Delbert?"

"Oh, yeah. You know how it is. Don't move quite as fast anymore."

"Don't I know it."

Marvin was a little younger than Delbert and he could see how Delbert was looking a little older than he remembered. Patrick had noticed it as well and was thinking about the future. He had someone in mind. So did his wife.

The Elephant In The Room

"Do you know for sure?"

"No, I can't say that I do."

"Mom, I wish you would have asked me before you sent the list. Or at least told me he was on the list."

"Well… I thought you would probably notice… and if you didn't want to send him an invitation… well… you wouldn't." She looked over at Angela and placed her hand on Angela's shoulder. "I am so sorry."

Angela didn't want to argue with her mother and hated the feelings she had about Glenn, but they were still there.

Later when they were alone, Noel asked, "Are you ever going to tell me about what happened with you and your brother?"

Angela bit on a fingernail and said, "I suppose it is about time. Let's go for a ride."

She had already told Noel how Glenn had his wild side growing up with stealing and shoplifting. In high school he got in the wrong crowd and was drinking a lot and on the verge of getting into drugs.

She hadn't told him about when she was in high school, just a sophomore. Angela said, "In order to pay for the drugs he was using he insinuated to his… whatever you want to call him, uh… his pusher… his dealer… that if push came to shove… well, he had a 'hot' sister that… you know, might be able to… " she took a deep sigh, "pay him for the drugs and… uh… not with money." She looked at Noel. "You know what I mean?"

Noel gave a serious and shocked look. "You mean, he was putting you out there for the guy to …?

"Yeah, that's what I am saying. Whatever he wanted to do with me, Glenn gave the impression I was available."

Hakeman's

A very well-dressed woman came into the store. She was slim, wore a dress, and heels. Her makeup was perfect. Not a hair out of place. And a smile that looked gracious, not at all fake.

Arlene returned the smile and said, "Tracy, good to see you. How are things going on the other side of the park?" Somewhere along the years businesses had a friendly rivalry going on. Businesses on one side of the park versus those on the other.

"Pretty good. Pretty good." Tracy smiled. "I always enjoy coming over here. Can't ever seem to leave without buying something."

"Well, that's what we like."

"Except for today."

"Today? Why?"

"I am here to see Brian. Is he around?"

"He just stepped out. Had to go home for something." Arlene was puzzled by the comments. "Can I help you?"

"No, I need to talk with Brian. Could you have him either call or come over to the store when he has time?"

"Sure. Will let him know."

"Thanks." And she was gone.

"I wonder what in the world she wants to talk to Brian about."

Eventide

Brian and Arlene

The two hadn't gone out together for a long time. One of the reasons was that they were saving their money for the future. But they did spend time together at Pop's with Jared and Brenda or just by themselves. And they were comfortable with that.

So, when Brian asked her if she would like to go out she was a little surprised. Of course, during Eventide, Fridays and Saturdays were out of the question since stores were open both nights.

Brian got reservations for Wednesday night and to their surprise The Dock was pretty busy. They both left from work and enjoyed the short jaunt out to Jewel Lake. Christmas decorations were seen everywhere.

“This place looks beautiful, doesn’t it?” She couldn’t remember The Dock looking prettier than it did now.

Brian smiled, “Yeah, it looks pretty nice.” They were holding hands as always when they were together. He hung up both coats and they were greeted by the hostess. Brian held Arlene’s chair as she sat down.

“Well, don’t get me wrong, but is this a special occasion or … what? I mean, we haven’t been out for a long time. Not that I mind. But, just curious.”

Brian smiled, “Oh, I don’t know. I just thought it was about time to go out, do something special. Maybe that will lift our spirits. That okay?”

Arlene raised her eyebrows and responded, “Sure, anytime. I love being with you and going out to someplace like this makes it all the better.” She put her hand over Brian’s.

Brian bit his bottom lip and confessed. “I do have a special reason for asking you out tonight. Uh… will talk about that later. Okay?”

“Well, now you’ve got me curious. How much later?”

“Let’s order first and then maybe we can talk about it.”

Eventide

The Night Continues

"Okay, Mr. Seagren, you can't say something like that and expect me to eat a meal before you tell me what you are up to. Spill it!"

Brian rubbed his chin and looked into her beautiful eyes. He adored everything about her. He would do anything for her. And now, as she sat there, he hoped that he was going about everything in the right way.

"Arlene, I've been thinking about us... a lot." He looked at her and then took her hand. "And I've been wanting to talk about our future."

"I think about you all the time as well."

Brian took a deep breath and said, "I would like to talk to your Dad, sometime. Do you think that would be okay?"

"Talk to my Dad? What about?" Arlene looked puzzled.

"Um... well..." he was having a hard time spitting it out. "I was going to ask him, uh... if we could get married."

Arlene wasn't expecting that. Her mouth was open as she just stared at Brian. Yes, she thought they would probably get married, and she was thinking he would give her a ring, possibly for Christmas but now that he said what he did, she didn't know how to respond. Add to that the fact that Arlene and her Dad weren't getting along too well lately because of something he said.

Arlene looked down and then looked back up at him and asked. "Brian, you know how he feels and yet you want to ask him if we can get married. Are you crazy? What are you thinking?"

"I am thinking that if I show him respect, by asking for permission that... that he might think... well... he might change his mind."

Arlene said, "I don't know if that is a good idea or not." Then she asked, "What if he says no? What then?"

"I don't know."

"Do you think your parents would be okay with us getting married?"

"Of course!" He answered, "Why wouldn't they?"

"Maybe they would think we were too young like my Dad does."

Brian gave her a blank stare at first. "Too young? Really?"

"Yeah." Arlene looked at him.

"I never considered that." Brian was truthful.

"Hey," Arlene said, "That doesn't mean I think we are too young."

Brian's feelings were relieved to hear Arlene say that. He smiled. "Good. I don't think we are either." He hesitated and then asked, "So, what about your Dad?"

This was indeed a question that needed to be resolved.

The Rehearsal

As it goes with most wedding rehearsals, not everyone shows up on time. You are always waiting for a groomsman, or a flower girl, or the soloist. Still, the basic rehearsal doesn't take long. And if things don't always go the way you planned, well, it is what it is.

It was the first time the two families got together. Angela had met only a few people in the family and today she was getting a huge dose of how many there were! Along with that, she was amazed at how wealthy they appeared to be.

In spite of their wealth, they were all very down to earth. Not even close to being pretentious, everyone got along very well. Speeches were given. Pictures were taken. Gifts handed out. The night ended with everyone being told not to party too much and to make it to the church on time!

On the way back to Emerald, Noel pulled Angela close. "Feeling okay about tomorrow?"

"You mean when I have a name change from Angela Hakeman to Angela Dahlke?"

"Yeah," he smiled, "something like that."

"I think so."

"I thought everything went pretty well, tonight."

Angela said, "I do too. And I think everything will go just as fine tomorrow."

He didn't know if he should bring it up. But he did. "So you don't think your brother is going to show up." He wondered how she would respond.

"No I don't. And even if he did. Nothing is going to spoil tomorrow."

"Wow!" Noel said, "I didn't expect that. I am glad you feel that way."

She smiled and said, "I am too."

Both really wondered what tomorrow might bring.

Richards Clothing

The customer leaving saw him coming and held the door for him. "Thanks!" The smell of new clothes was everywhere. Soft music playing in the background. Several men were looking at suits and sport jackets. That was on the right.

On the left women were looking for dresses, blouses, and slacks. One of the women in that area noticed Brian enter and immediately headed his way.

"Thanks for coming Brian." Tracy shook his hand.

Brian smiled, "No problem. Arlene said you wanted to see me."

"Yes, do you have time to talk?"

"Sure. I don't have to be back at Hakeman's for a while." He nervously scratched behind his ear. "What did you want to see me about... exactly?"

Tracy smiled at him. "Well, I was talking with Angela Hakeman, and she told me you were working for her while Shirley was ... well... until Shirley can come back to work. Right?"

"Yeah. Right now it is just for a couple of weeks more, until Angela gets back from her honeymoon."

"Well, Angela has only good things to say about you and I was wondering if you had anything lined up for the rest of the summer."

Brian bluntly said, "Not really. Finding work is harder than I thought it would be. Why?"

"Well, we are looking for someone to work in the Men's department and we were wondering if you would be interested."

"Selling suits, that kind of thing?"

"Exactly!"

"I really don't know anything about that."

"We would teach you."

"Gosh, I don't know. I mean, I am flattered. I guess I should jump at the chance. But..."

Tracy smiled, "Why don't you talk to my husband. Better yet, why don't you talk to my father-in-law, Delbert. He can tell you a lot about what the job entails."

And a time was set up for the two to get together. This would be the beginning of something big for Brian. And he didn't know it... yet.

Wedding Day

Rain was not in the forecast for today. And for once, the weatherman was in the win column, which doesn't happen all that often. There were enough clouds, the white puffy kind, to give brilliance to the blue sky.

Late afternoon was when the wedding was to take place. Everything was going according to schedule. Hakeman's would close at 3:00 p.m. so Arlene and Brian could be in attendance.

Angela and Noel decided to go with tradition and didn't see one another before she walked down the aisle. The church was three quarters full. Noel's family outnumbered Angela's but the people in Emerald filled in so both sides looked about the same number.

Everything went without a hitch. And then when it was official and there was a Mr. and Mrs. Noel Dahlke, they headed toward the area where the reception line would be formed. This was a very traditional wedding, just what they wanted.

Brian and Arlene sat together and held hands most of the time. Arlene was watching Michael and Daniel as they were taking pictures and she wondered two things. She wondered if she would be doing this kind of thing someday, taking pictures. She also wondered what her wedding would be like and when it would be.

They were about to head toward the reception hall. Angela was looking all over for her parents, but she didn't see them anywhere. Where could they be. "Oh well," she thought, "I will see them at the reception. Maybe they are there already."

As Noel and Angela got in their limo, and headed for the hall, Angela saw her parents talking to someone she didn't recognize. "Probably someone from Noel's family," she thought.

The rest of the day flew by. Ultimately, they ended up in Bermuda where they spent the week. Life was good.

Job #2

Shirley Nieting was getting back to feeling her old self. The symptoms of MS subsided a little. Walking was easier. She hadn't fallen in some time, and she was feeling stronger. Getting back to work was on her mind.

And it seemed to work out perfectly. Brian knew the original plan was for him to work through June. His job offer at Richards Clothing came at just the right time.

"So," Jared asked, "you're going to be selling clothes now, huh."

The two couples were enjoying a pizza at Pop's.

"Yeah, it looks like it."

And then Arlene added, "And he gets a discount when he needs new clothes." She smiled at Brian. "And he looks good in new clothes."

Brenda asked, "Does his girlfriend get a discount?"

"I don't know," Arlene responded. She looked at Brian, "Does she?"

He stared back at her. "I don't know. I will have to find out."

Jared asked, "You think you'll like it?"

"I think so," Brian pulled a piece onto his plate. "Delbert, Patrick's Dad has been teaching me a little about selling suits and the like. I like him. He reminds me of my Grandpa. I don't always get his sense of humor. But I didn't always get Grandpa Seagren's sense of humor either."

"How's the pay?"

"Bout the same as Hakeman's."

"Is it just for the summer?"

"No. I get the impression that this is going to be full-time if I want it."

"So you are thinking about NOT going to college with me?" Arlene asked. She was a little surprised.

"I don't know. I have been thinking about... well, I don't know."

You could tell that Arlene wasn't sure about what she had just found out. She got quiet. She didn't know how she felt. She would have to give this some thought.

Picnic Time

When the Fourth of July arrives, you realize it is all downhill now before fall makes its entrance. The excitement of the area moves from Emerald to Jewel Lake.

The Kemps and the Emeralds enjoy their time on Fred's pontoon. Arlene remembers, vaguely, the time Jake invited her to view the fireworks from that vantage point.

Nancy Cooper gets to be pulled around the lake skiing until it gets too crowded. Phil and Evelyn Jordan are watching her show off her skills. And then she goes down.

Jared, Brenda, Brian, and Arlene are spending the day together. No secret hideaway but they have claimed a table in the state park for their meal. The shelter house serves as the meeting point for a family reunion this year. Everyone has to fend for their own.

Jared and Brian head down to the beach giving Brenda and Arlene time to talk.

"How are you doing Arlene?"

"Fine. Why do you ask?"

"Well, the last time we were together, and you found out Brian might not be going back to college, you got kind of quiet."

"Well," she defended her actions, "that was the first I heard of it. I mean, he talked about it, but I didn't know he made a decision."

"How do you feel now?"

"I guess I'm okay with it." She looked down. "I just think about our future together. I do that a lot. Having him around all the time is like a dream come true, But..."

"But what?"

"Can I tell you something Brenda?"

"You always do."

"I've got wedding fever."

"Wedding fever?"

"Yeah, wedding fever. And I've got it bad."

"What brought this on?"

"Well, I have had it for quite a while. And then, Angela's wedding didn't help any. She was so beautiful and..."

Brenda interrupted, "Does Brian know you have wedding fever?"

"Probably. I don't know." And then Arlene asked, "Don't you have that... feeling... desire... or whatever with Jared?"

"Yes, I guess I do but I am also looking at things practically and financially. We are saving up so we can have a nice little nest egg when the time comes."

"Saving up?"

"Yeah."

"What are you two talking about?" The guys had come back.

A Post Wedding Surprise

All the gifts were stacked in the living room, waiting for Noel and Angela to open. They got quite a haul. Coming back from Bermuda, everything was different. No more, "See you tomorrow." Living together was something they both longed for.

When the Fourth arrived they didn't even consider going to the lake. How could it compare to Bermuda? Instead they decided to spend a quiet time at home. Noel fired up the grill for hot dogs and hamburgers. Potato salad was already in the fridge. Opening presents would be a priority. Sending "thank you" cards would also start, but not today.

Since both had been living separately and basically had what they needed as far as cooking ware was concerned, it would be a challenge to think of what kind of gift people could purchase. And so they decided to register at several places in Alcoa. Ultimately, from the looks of things, most decided to give cash or gift cards. The box for cards was almost full.

"Well, we didn't get any duplicates."

"Yeah, that is the good thing. But what do you suppose this is?" Noel held up something he had never seen before.

"Yeah, that has me puzzled too. Who gave that to us?"

"It says, the Samuelson's."

"Friends of yours?"

"Never heard of them. Thought they were your friends."

This was one gift where they would have to do some investigating. But that would wait. On to the box of cards. Angela opened the cards and read them. Noel recorded who gave what.

Everything was going smoothly and then about a third of the way through the box, everything came to a halt. It didn't start that way. In fact, Angela read the outside of the card where a message was printed. It said, "You were a beautiful bride!" Angela kidded, "Well someone has good taste. Let's see who this is from." Inside there were two one-hundred-dollar bills and a letter. She started to silently read what someone took the time to write.

Reading the expression on her face, Noel could tell this wasn't a letter she appreciated. After reading just a few lines she went to the end of the letter to see who signed it. Seeing the signature she took a deep breath, put her fist to her mouth and looked away.

"Uh, not good?" Noel asked. "Who was it from?"

She handed the letter to Noel. He read the signature: Glenn Hakeman.

A Phone Call

After all the niceties were exchanged, Angela got down to the reason for the call. "Mom, did you know Glenn was at the wedding?"

Joanie was hesitant to say anything, but she felt she had to. "Yes, I knew he was there."

"Did you talk to him?"

"Yes, but it wasn't until after the ceremony. We didn't see him until we went outside the church. He was waiting for us."

"Why didn't you say something to me?"

"Well," Joanie was trying to explain, "I was going to, but I didn't want to upset you. And I guess he didn't want to upset you either. He didn't want us to say anything." There was silence for a bit before Joanie continued. "How did you find out he was there?"

"He gave us a card with two hundred dollars in it along with a letter."

"Two hundred dollars! Wow! That is quite a gift!"

"Yes it was."

"How do you feel about that?"

Angela was slow to reply. "To be honest with you Mom, I really don't know. I am angry and then… I just don't know."

"Angela, he is really sorry for what he did in the past. I think if you two would just sit down and talk, well… it would help a lot."

"I don't know if I am ready to talk. I have to go. I'll talk to you later."

Letting It All Out

Noel was listening to the whole conversation. "Ange, can we talk more about this whole thing with your brother?"

She looked at him, sighed, and said, "Yeah, let's get it all in the open." She put her hands together on the table, tilted her head back, looked at the ceiling and began.

"I told you he was into drugs, and he owed money to the guy supplying the drugs."

"Yeah, I remember you said he told the guy that you were available to …"

"Yeah, he kind of pimped me out. Or, tried to."

"That must have been scary."

"It was. I was just in high school, and this creepy guy seemed to be wherever I wanted to be."

"Did he talk to you?"

"Yeah, he tried to act cool and wanted me to go out with him. He told me Glenn would vouch for him and we would have a great time together. Noel, he was disgusting. I told him no over and over again. And then after a while he got tired of me saying no. He said if I didn't go out with him, someone was going to get hurt."

"Wow. What did he mean by that?"

"I don't know but that scared me. And I tried never to be anywhere by myself after that."

"Did you talk to Glenn about him?"

"You bet I did. I told him to tell his creepy friend to stay away from me."

"What did Glenn say?"

"He said he was a nice guy and that I should go out with him."

"Really?"

"Yeah."

"And did you?"

"Look, I was in high school, and I didn't know what to do. Finally, I gave in, kind of." She looked to the side before continuing. "I told him I would be out at the state park for a picnic and if he was there we could get away and talk for a while."

"Did he go for that?"

"Yeah, he did."

"And?"

"And we walked around together for a while and talked. He was friendly and seemed nicer than he was before. And so we went down by the beach, a little ways from the dock where there weren't as many people. We sat together, not real close at first. But that changed. I guess I didn't mind that he scooted over next to me. And then..."

"Then what?"

"Well, he put his hand to my face and turned my head to look at him and he was going to kiss me."

"Did you let him?"

"I wasn't going to. But I had never been kissed before. And he was saying nice things to me, and I thought I wanted to see what it was like to be kissed. So I let him kiss me."

"And?"

"And he smelled like cigarettes. It was a real turnoff. But that wasn't the worst part."

"No. As he was kissing me, his hand went from my face to my chest. He tried to feel my breast. When I tried to stop him he got this surprised look on his face and said, 'What?'"

"Did you tell Glenn what he tried to do?"

"Yes and Glenn said... I don't remember what he said but he got a scared look. I think he knew the guy was going to do what he did and probably try to do more. I don't know."

"Wow!"

"And ever since that time, we have never said much of anything to each other."

A Revisited Time

Angela put her head down on the table.

"I am so sorry that happened to you. I had no idea."

"I know you didn't. Until now, no one else knows the story, not even my parents."

"You didn't tell them?"

"No. I was so embarrassed about what happened, that he would touch me like that. And that my brother thought I would be okay with that."

"Ange, what did the letter say?"

"Read it for yourself." She handed it to him.

He read it for himself over the next few minutes. Putting it down, Noel just sat there for a few minutes. Then he looked at Angela. "So, do you believe him?"

"I don't know."

"He sounds sincere. I mean I don't know the guy. But he brought everything out in the open, at least as far as I can tell. He doesn't try to defend himself. He must have really been messed up."

"He was."

"But now... now it sounds like he has changed and wants to make amends." They looked at one another and Noel asked, "Are you going to make contact with him?"

Taking a deep breath she answered, "I don't know. Hold me. Would you just hold me right now Noel."

Family Discussion

Brian knew he had to talk to his parents about what he was thinking. He had a similar discussion when he said he didn't want to go back to Iowa City. They were surprised but didn't say much. At that time he was looking toward attending college at Alcoa.

They knew about the relationship he had with Arlene and smiled thinking about what his real thoughts were. But now, well, this was different.

"Mom, Dad, I've been doing a lot of thinking about this fall."

"Okay," his Mom began, "what about this fall."

Brian took a deep breath and said, "I don't know if I want to go to Alcoa Junior College or not."

"I thought that was your plan. You seemed excited about going there with Arlene, driving together. Have you two broken up?"

"No. Nothing like that. I don't know. I am just not that interested in school anymore."

"Well, what would you do?"

"I was thinking of continuing to work at Richards Clothing. They are really happy with me. They told me that. And I got my first raise."

"Are you planning on working there the rest of your life?"

"I don't know. Probably not. Maybe. I just don't know."

His Mom was asking all the questions. Dad just sat there listening and wondering how much of this had to do with Arlene. But he didn't ask that question. He let his wife do that.

"Does this have anything to do with Arlene?"

"Maybe. I don't know." He started to stumble with his words. "You know I gave Arlene that Promise Ring. Well, I meant it when I gave it to her and ... I don't know."

"Are you two planning on getting married?" His Mom now had a very concerned look.

"Well, I haven't asked her if that's what you mean. But, yeah, I think that will happen... someday."

His Mom looked at his Dad, who didn't look back at her. He kind of smiled to himself, knowing the anguish his son was going through.

His Mom continued. "Well, we like Arlene. She is a very nice young woman. She is pretty and carries herself very well. She is always so polite in Hakeman's but..."

"But what?"

"Aren't you a little young to get married? And how will you support yourselves?"

This wasn't going the way Brian thought it would and the discussion was starting to wind down. Brian said, "I was just thinking about it." He picked up his jacket and went out the door.

His Dad smiled as he looked at his wife. "A little young? Really? How old were we when we got married?"

All she said was, "That was different."

"Right!" He went back to reading his paper.

Boyfriend/Girlfriend Discussion

She knew it was him. She could tell how his car sounded. And she was used to him coming over almost any time. He felt comfortable around her parents. And her parents liked him. They thought of him as being very responsible and focused in life.

She went out the front door before he even got to the sidewalk. "Hi Brian." She could tell he wasn't in the best of moods by the expression on his face. She asked, "What's wrong?"

"Got time to go for a walk?"

"Sure. Let me tell Mom what we're doing." She went in the house, and he could hear her yelling, "Brian and I are going for a walk. Be back later!" He didn't hear any response. "So," grabbing his hand she asked, "What's up?"

"Well, had a discussion with my parents a little while ago."

"Didn't go too well?" Arlene asked.

"You could say that."

"What was it about?"

"I told them I was thinking about NOT going back to school this fall. Then I told them I was thinking about working at Richards Clothing. You know I got that raise and everything."

"Yeah. What did they say?"

"Well," and he hesitated, "it was Mom that had all the questions. She asked if you had anything to do with my decision."

"What did you say?"

"I told her that you probably did. Because you do! Anything I do I do thinking about you and … us. And then she asked if we were getting married."

"Is she okay with that? I mean I thought she liked me."

"She does. She does. But they think we are too young."

They walked along in silence for a while. They took turns squeezing each other's hand.

What Are We Going To Do?

"I think we need to put together a plan."

"A plan?"

"Yeah. We need to plan out our future and show it to our parents, let them see we are responsible."

"That sounds like a good idea... maybe."

Arlene said, "And we should put it down on paper so we can review it and change it." She was getting excited about the prospect of putting the plan together.

They found a booth out at Pop's, sat down on the same side. Arlene had a pencil and pad. At the top of the page she wrote Arlene and Brian's Plan.

"Okay. Number one will be that you continue to work at Richards Clothing making as much money as you can, getting raise after raise. At the same time I will finish my studies regarding photography."

Brian asked, "Do you think you will start your own studio?"

"I don't know but that is a definite possibility. I might see if I can use part of the Examiners space to set it up. You know, like that ice cream place took part of the hardware store."

"Sure, that sounds good. I wonder how much it would cost to start up."

"I don't know but Michael could give me some suggestions on that."

"Sounds good. So what's next?"

Arlene thought for a minute, biting her bottom lip. "Well, if I have to I can work at Hakeman's. I am sure that Angela would let me. And if I work full time I bet she would increase my pay." And getting excited about that she said, "And I could save as much as I can, like you."

"Okay. Okay. Okay. We need to find out how much it costs to rent an apartment and utilities and all those things."

"Yeah, and then we need to put together a budget and see if we can make enough to take care of all the bills."

"And save, save, SAVE!"

They were both getting excited about what they were doing, thinking of their future together.

Arlene said, "And then, well you know, after we are married we will have to plan for, you know, when that time comes..."

"What time?"

"You know... when we have kids." They both shared a smile.

"Oh, yeah." Brian leaned in for a kiss. At the same time she squeezed his thigh.

Talking with Brenda and Jared

"Your Mom said we would probably find you here." Brenda and Jared walked in and sat down across from Arlene and Brian.

"Mind if we join you?"

"Of course not. You can help us. Or maybe we can help you!"

"Okay, what are you two up too?"

"We just happen to be putting together a plan for our future." Arlene gave a smug look.

Jared looked at Brian, "You proposed!"

And Brenda immediately looked at Arlene's hand to see a ring.

"No, you moron. I didn't propose... yet." And Brian went on to explain the reaction he got from his parents concerning his not going to school this fall.

"Well, I can see why you are doing what you are doing. Can't say that it is a bad idea to put all those plans together. But do you think it will make a difference?"

Arlene answered, "Well, it can't hurt." And then she went on, "Hey, how about a little support here!"

Brenda spoke up. "Hey, we are supporting you. Really, we are." And then she looked at the pad. "What have you got so far?"

Arlene read it off and then asked, "What do you think?"

Brenda looked at Jared. "I think it sounds good. And you know when it comes to putting together a budget, I know just who to ask about that."

"Really? Who?"

"Jake and Rachael." Brenda let that sink in for a minute. They are getting married in a few weeks and I know they have tried to figure everything out, down to the penny.

Arlene surprised everyone when she said, "Let's do it. I will talk to Rachael as soon as I can."

Jared looked at Brian and said, "I think Arlene wants to get married very soon. Better watch out."

Arlene looked at Jared and kiddingly said, "Shut up Emerald." And then she grabbed Brian's arm and pulled it close to her.

In the back of her mind Brenda remembered how after a little champaign, how aggressive Arlene got.

A lot of things were going through the minds of each of this group of four.

Hakeman's

"Well, I for one, am glad to say you are not changing the name of the store." Shirley Nieting had times when she could be very adamant in what she said. "After all, Hakeman's is kind of an institution."

Angela smiled, "You know, actually, I never gave it a thought. What? We would call it Dahlke's? That doesn't sound right. No, it will always be Hakeman's."

Shirley had been back for a while, and it seemed like old times once again. Brian had done a good job and in fact it was because he did such a good job that Tracy Richards thought of hiring him. And did!

Angela looked up at the clock and then her wristwatch, purely out of habit and said, “Arlene should be in any time now.”

Shirley thought for a moment and then asked, “Seems to me Arlene was thinking of working for that gal in Alcoa, taking pictures. Whatever happened with that?”

“I’m not really sure. She was excited about that for a while, and I told her we could work around her hours there if she was really getting serious about doing that professionally.” After a quizzical look Angela continued, “Guess she changed her mind.”

“You think her boyfriend had anything to do with that?” Shirley smiled.

“I don’t know. But I wouldn’t be surprised.”

And then the phone rang. “Hakeman’s Cards and Things, this is Angela, how can I help you?”

It was her Mom.

News from Mom

“Angela, this is your Mom. How is married life?”

Angela couldn't see it, but her Mom had a huge smile on her face. "Oh, pretty good. Don't know why it took so long for it to happen."

"I am so glad to hear that. We really like Noel. And we enjoyed meeting his family. And I must say it is quite a family! Can't imagine having them all over for Thanksgiving or Christmas."

Angela smiled. "I don't think that is going to happen anytime soon. We'll have to see how the dynamics work out. Anyway, I like his family too. One brother is kind of wild and I think he was flirting with me a lot at the reception."

"Was that the brother that is just a little taller than Noel, slightly gray at the temples?"

"That's the one."

"Better watch out."

"I think I can handle him." Then she asked, "Any reason for the call. I mean, everything is okay isn't it?"

"Oh sure, just hadn't talked with you for a while." Then she asked, "Anything new with you and your brother? I mean after the gift and letter he wrote." There was silence for a while that made Joanie very uncomfortable. She asked, "Have... uh, you forgiven him?"

"Have I forgiven him?"

"Have you?" Joanie asked.

"Don't know that forgiveness is the word. Don't think that I ever thought of not forgiving him. You brought us up that way. Forgiveness was never an option you always told us. You always forgive. I guess I was...am... I don't know, just upset at what he did. Do you understand?"

"I am so glad to hear you say that." Joanie said. "Do you want his number so you can call him?"

"Well, maybe sometime in the future. Not right now. That okay?"

"Sure. Well I better let you go. I think your Dad is getting ready to go to town?"

And this interesting phone call came to an end.

Lunch With Her

A booth was Arlene's choice for this meeting. She wanted privacy. Not that what she was asking for was scandalous or anything like that. But it was personal.

Arlene asked Angela if she could be a little late. She didn't know how it would go. No problem. Shirley could stay a little later if need be.

Arlene was dressed for work and as the fall was becoming more and more apparent of its arrival, Arlene found fashionable clothes to complement her. She felt very good about her appearance.

She was pleased with the image she wanted to reveal. Since Brian ended up paying for them, they got a discount!

When her lunch partner appeared, she was dressed in a similar fashion. And at one time Arlene would have been very jealous. But that time had long passed. Anyone seeing these two having lunch would see two very attractive young ladies that would always get a ... second look.

"Hi." They both said it almost at the same time.

"I am so glad you have the time to have lunch with me. I know this is a busy week for you and I hate to impose."

Rachael responded. "Please! I am so glad to take a break and think about something other than the wedding." By the end of the week Rachael Meadows would have a name change. She would become Mrs. Jake Emerald on Saturday. But this was Monday and she looked forward to the distraction.

Before they got their meal and to the questions Arlene had, Arlene asked, "You excited? I'll bet you are. How could you not be!"

Rachael looked away for a second and then said, "Yeah, I am excited." And then she looked at Arlene. "And I must say, I am kind of surprised that you are talking about it the way you are."

"You mean because of me and Jake and all that?"

"Yeah. Don't get me wrong but ... this is such a turnaround for you. And I like having you as a friend, but... you know."

"Yeah, I know what you mean. I'm glad we are friends too."

The meal had just arrived and so they spent some time in small talk. When Arlene thought that was enough she asked, "Got a question for you. Or maybe it is advice or... something like that."

"What is it?" Rachael took another bite waiting to hear what Arlene had to say.

"It is about living where you do."

"What do you want to know?"

"Well, I am curious about how much it costs. You know, like rent and utilities, that kind of thing."

"Why. Are you thinking of moving out on your own?"

Arlene thought she should have expected the question. She hadn't. Now how much did she want to share. "Well, uh... I don't know." And then she thought to herself, "Why not tell her."

"Promise me you won't say anything to anybody."

"Okay."

"Promise?"

"I promise."

Arlene looked around and bent over the table to get closer to Rachael. This was news the world didn't need to hear. "Brian and I are thinking about the future and are just wondering what it costs to live on our own."

Rachael's eyebrows went up, "You're engaged! That is wonderful. I am so happy for you."

Arlene waved off the comment. "No, we are not engaged but are looking towards the possibility sometime in the future and we want to ... I don't know...how do they say it? We just want to be prepared."

Rachael smiled. "I understand. I tell you what. I have a budget I follow every two weeks because I get paid every two weeks. I could make you a copy and you could get an idea of what the costs might be. How's that?"

"That would be perfect, just what we need to see."

Rachael gave a sly smile. "You really love this guy don't you?"

Arlene looked down, kind of embarrassed. Then she rolled her eyes and said, "I can't stop thinking about him."

"I know just the feeling."

Talking With Dad

Arlene's next move was to talk to her Dad about... well, she didn't know how she was going to bring it up, but she wanted to know how he felt about things.

She didn't have to go to school today and so she decided to visit her Dad at the Examiner.

"Hey sweetie. This is a surprise. What are you up to today?"

"Well, I had time to kill, and I thought I would come over and talk to you for a while. You have time?"

"I always have time for my princess." He motioned to a chair and then sat down himself. Looking at her he smiled, "I can't get over how much you've changed over just the last year. You look so mature, not that little girl I once knew."

She was glad to hear him say that. Maybe he would think she was old enough to move to that next step she and Brian were thinking about. "Well, thank you Daddy. But remember, I will always be your little girl."

"I hope so."

"Daddy, I have a question for you." He just sat there and waited. "Uh, Brian and I, well, we have been dating a while now." She was looking down as she spoke. "And he gave me this Promise Ring a while back. But you know that." Still looking down but looking around on the floor for the words she wanted to say and the courage to say them. "Uh, we are thinking about the future."

George interrupted her. "You two getting serious?"

It scared her that he asked it the way he did. "Yeah, Daddy, we are." There she said it. And after she said it her Dad rubbed his chin and stood up, walking around a little.

"What are you thinking? Does this have anything to do with Jake and Rachael getting married?"

"No! It has nothing to do with them. At all!" Arlene couldn't fathom why he would think that. Well, maybe a little. "I don't think about Jake anymore. Haven't for a while. And I am happy for Jake and Rachael. Real happy. This has to do with just me and Brian."

Her Dad rubbed his neck. "I don't know sweetie. You two are awfully young."

"You just said how mature I am now! You said it yourself."

"I know. I know. And you are. But getting married? Oh, sweetie I don't know." And before he could think about what he was saying he asked, "You aren't in trouble are you?"

Arlene's mouth fell open. At first she didn't know what to say. And then she looked at her father and said, "Daddy! You think I am pregnant?" She shook her head, looked down and then looked him the eye and said, " How could you? How could you?" Her eyes got big. Her face got red, and then she started to shake her head as if she couldn't believe what he said. She started to cry and then left the office.

There wasn't a thing he could do to remedy the situation.

Not a good day for either.

A Lot of Happiness

Married life suited them just fine. And that could be said for the two couples Arlene had witnessed saying their vows over the last few months.

Jake and Rachael had been Jake and Rachael for a long time. Everyone saw it coming with these two. And with Jake and Rachael now both working out at The Dock, Jake full-time and Rachael, every so often, their life looked perfect.

And Noel and Ange, she had become accustomed to him now calling her Ange. Well, not all the time. But that is how Noel referred to her and he was in the store at least once every day. They looked like the perfect couple.

They were in the process of making Angela's home, their home. In other words they were putting money into it. Nothing had actually been spent as of yet, but the plans were there: painting, new flooring, adding another bathroom, new cupboards. A total remake was in order.

Angela seemed to always be wearing a smile. Life was good for her. Hakeman's was doing really well. Her employees deserved raises and they got them. They worked hard and took ownership of the place.

As far as Arlene was concerned and even though she was still, technically, part-time since she had school to finish, she got a generous increase in her pay too. And a good portion was put away into savings. Savings for what, she wasn't sure anymore. But right now it was tucked away in a special account at Emerald State Bank.

A Lot of Sadness

But there is also the reverse. Ever since Arlene had that conversation with her Dad and Brian had with basically his Mom, they were both uncertain about how their parents would respond to them getting married. Or, even just engaged!

Arlene left the Examiner that morning crying. She tried to hide it but was having a tough time doing that. To have her Dad ask her that question, it was like a ton of bricks falling on her. They had such a close relationship, and then he went and asked something so personal, thinking that she had... it broke her heart.

What could she do? Who could she talk to? Brenda? Yes, but she was working. Brian? Same scenario. She decided to get in the car and go to the city park and just cry.

Things weren't any better in the Examiner office. George wanted to say something to Arlene before she left crying but didn't know what to say. He watched her break down and he wanted to take it all back. Why? Why in the world would he ask such a question? He knew he had gone too far. And to see the look in her eyes. He knew it crushed her.

His head in his hands, he started to cry as well. How could he do that to his pride and joy. He was always so proud of her. And now, now he didn't know what the future would look like or how long it would take to resolve this issue. Had his stupid question driven her away for good? He didn't know.

Right now there was a lot of sadness. And it would spread as the story got around.

Sunglasses

She sat in the park with the car window down. She was dry of tears by this time, but confusion was still stuck in her mind. Her eyes were red and puffy. She didn't want anyone to see her like this. But she needed to talk to somebody. And that somebody was Brenda. This was a Brenda sized problem.

She looked through the car to see if she left her sunglasses ... somewhere. She hoped she had. She didn't have her purse with her. That is where they were quite often. Finally she found them. Looking in the mirror she wondered if anyone could see that she had been crying. Maybe? At this point she didn't care.

Brenda was restocking a shelf with macaroni and cheese when she noticed Arlene, clad in sunglasses coming down the aisle. Arlene leaned down. "I need to talk with you." Without waiting for a response, she almost dragged Brenda out the back door.

"So what is up?"

Arlene took her glasses off and Brenda could see she had been crying.

"Oh, no, Arlene. What happened?"

Arlene let it all out. She told Brenda everything. What she said. What her Dad asked. Everything.

Brenda didn't say a word. She just listened. They were both leaning against a car parked in back.

After a few minutes of silence, Arlene asked, "What am I going to do?"

"I don't know. I just can't imagine your Dad thinking you and Brian, you know..."

"Me either."

"Have you told Brian?"

"No. You are the first one." She was holding her sunglasses in her hands. Her eyes weren't quite as red and puffy. "Should I tell Brian?"

"I don't know," Brenda said, not looking at Arlene. "Maybe you should."

"Would you tell Jared if your Dad asked you that question?"

"Tough one. I don't know." Then Brenda said, "I think Brian needs to know. Maybe he can say something that will... I don't know... make you feel better?" She said it like it was a question.

"Well, I have to go to work soon. I need to get home and get cleaned up, put some makeup on and get a smiley face like everything is fine. But I sure don't feel like it."

"Why don't you call Richards Clothing and see if you and Brian can get together after work. Go to Pop's or someplace."

Arlene thought about that and said, "Yeah, that sounds good. I sure don't want to go home for supper."

"You want me and Jared to come?"

"I don't know. Maybe later, say, maybe at seven?"

"We'll be there."

Pop's

Brian had no idea what he was in for. He was just glad to be with Arlene as much as he could. And Pop's was one place they really liked to hang out.

He had parked next to the shelter house right across from the store and decided to walk over to Hakeman's and walk back with Arlene.

He didn't get in the store. She came out, gave him a smile, and took his hand. "Have a good day?" he asked.

"Um, not so much."

"What happened?"

"I will tell you over supper."

As they had been saving their money, having supper was one of those things they didn't do very often. Something bad must have happened.

Well, supper didn't really happen. Arlene wasn't all that hungry and so they just got pop and some pizza bites to munch on. Brian didn't say a whole lot. He just basically listened to Arlene explain what her morning had been like. When she finished, Brian just sat there.

Finally Brian said, "Wow!" Not much of an expression on his face he went on to say, "So your Dad thinks that we have ..."

Arlene looked at Brian with no expression at all and said, "Yeah. I guess he does."

"Wow!"

Jared and Brenda came over to their booth, saw the sad faces and didn't say anything at first. Then Brenda said, "Hope you don't mind but I filled Jared in on what happened."

"I don't mind. I don't care. I am just so depressed."

With caring eyes, Brenda looked over at her friend. She put her hand over Arlene's. They looked like they had just heard a good friend died.

Jared was the one who broke the silence. "Well, now what?"

No one said anything at first.

Arlene made the drastic statement. “Well, my life is over. How can I ever face my Dad?”

Brian immediately said, “Whoa, whoa, wait a minute. What about me? What about us?” No reply. “I mean, don’t get me wrong. What your Dad said hurt you. I understand that, but maybe... I don’t know, maybe he is sad he said that.”

“You’re taking his side!???”

“Never!” Brian quickly replied. “Arlene, I love you and I want to always be with you. And I hope deep in my heart that you feel the same way. But I also know you adored your father, and your father adored you. And then this morning happened.” He ran out of things to say and so he concluded, “I don’t know.”

It had been an exhausting day. No one knew what the future held in store.

Hakeman’s

October had come and gone. And things had settled down somewhat with ... everyone. Then again, nothing really had changed on the Brian and Arlene front.

Noel and Ange were going strong. Everyday seemed to hold

something new and exciting. And Ange brought that excitement to the store as everyone was getting excited about Eventide.

"I am so glad that last shipment finally came in and that everything was still intact."

"I know. Those items are really fragile. But they were packed like they should be. Getting them replaced might not have happened until ... I don't know, Emerald Days?"

Even Arlene was enjoying the mood in the store. She loved the fall with the cooler temperatures and shorter days. A lot of people don't care for it much, but she wasn't one of them.

The home scene for her was what it was. Not a lot of joy. But when she got to work or was with Brian, it was a different story.

"Are we going to do the same as last year, with the partitions and everything?"

"I think so," Angela said with a smile and a nodding of the head. "I think people might even expect it. That was fun last year, wasn't it?"

Arlene spoke up, "I thought it was."

Shirley kidded her a little, "That was because Brian was standing right next to you all night."

"Was not!" Arlene teased back as if she was talking to Brenda.

Angela was really enjoying everything. She was married to the love of her life. She had a successful business. She was getting to the point of having a beautiful home. And then the phone rang.

Bad to Worse

The bantering back and forth continued for a while, and everyone enjoyed just being together. As she went to answer the phone, she had a smile on her face and a hint of joy in her voice, “Hakeman’s, this is Angela, how can I help you?”

At first there was silence. “Hello. Hello. Is anyone there?” Then she heard a sniffle. Again she said, “Hello.”

In what sounded like someone trying to catch their breath, Angela heard a weak voice saying, “Angela is that you?” She didn’t recognize who was calling.

“Yes, this is Angela Dahlke, who is this?’

“It’s your mother Angela, I have some bad news.”

Immediately she thought about her Dad. “What happened? Is Dad okay?”

“No. No he is not.”

“What happened?”

Joanie tried to gather herself together before she continued. “He was coming home from town and… and they don’t know for sure what happened but he ran off the road and hit a tree."

"Oh no!" Angela turned pale. "Is he okay? Did they take him to the hospital? Is he home?" She knew by the sound of her mom's voice nothing positive was going to be in her response.

Shirley and Arlene were hearing snippets of what was being said and came into the back room to hear more.

"He's in the hospital. I am here too. Angela, it doesn't look good."

"What do you mean it doesn't look good?"

She sniffled a little. "He's on life support right now. He could go at any time."

Angela closed her eyes. Just a few months ago they had all been together at the wedding. A lot of joy and happiness. Now that looked like the last time they would all be together.

"Oh, Mom. What can I do?" Typical question.

"Nothing. You can't do anything. Pastor is here with me along with a friend from church. They are wonderful."

Angela was happy her Mom wasn't alone.

"But I have a favor to ask."

"Anything."

"That number I gave you for Glenn. Would you please call him and let him know what has happened. I don't have the number here."

Angela said, "Of course. Of course."

A Big Surprise

Angela could hardly refuse her devastated mom. Joanie had sent her the number to get hold of Glenn. She had the number at home in an address book. She never thought about ever calling him. Guess that idea went out the window.

"I have to leave."

Both Shirley and Arlene said, "Go! Go!" They would take care of everything at the store. When sad news comes, everyone else is as accommodating as they can be. Suddenly, no matter what you are going through, what someone else is going through is much worse.

She called Noel at work, and he came home immediately. She explained what had happened to her father.

"Should we take off for the hospital?"

"I don't think it will do any good. I don't think he has much time left." She explained who was with her mom. "We need to find that letter with Glenn's phone number."

"You have Glenn's number?"

"Yes, don't you remember. Mom insisted that I have it handy, you know, just in case."

"I remember but I thought you threw that letter away."

"I didn't. It is in my address book. At least I hope it is." She frantically tried to find the address book. She didn't use it that often. "Help me find it. PLEASE!"

Noel was just standing there but now was looking feverishly or at least look like it. "Ange, what does it look like?"

"A red cover ADDRESS BOOK written in gold letters."

"Found it."

"Where was it?"

"Junk drawer."

She started to page through it looking for a letter. There was more than one. "Got it," she yelled.

She sat down and dialed the number. One ring. Two rings. This is Joplin Police Department, Seargeant Brisco speaking, how can I help you?"

Angela immediately thought, "Oh, no. Our Dad is dying, and Glenn is in jail. Great! Well, maybe not. Maybe I got the wrong number." She asked, "I'm sorry to bother you. I may have gotten the wrong number. I was looking for Glenn Hakeman." And then she went on to say, "Maybe he is in your jail?"

"In jail?" was the response she got. "Why would Detective Hakeman be in jail?"

Detective Hakeman

"My brother is a cop? More than that, he is a Detective? When did that happen? And why didn't anyone tell me?" Those were her first thoughts.

She responded to the Sargeant. "I guess... I mean... is Detective Hakeman there?"

"Sorry, not right now. Can I take a message and have him get back to you?"

"Uh, yeah, this is his sister Angela Dahlke. I just heard from my Mom. Our Dad was in an accident, and it looks bad."

"So sorry to hear that Angela, I will let him know. Does he have your number?"

"I don't know. Probably not." She gave it to him.

Before he hung up he said, "By the way, congrats on your wedding. Detective Hakeman had great things to say about it. Said you were the most beautiful thing he had ever seen."

Angela didn't know what to say and so she said, "Uh, thanks."

She turned to Noel. "You won't believe what I have to say."

"No?"

"I don't know if I believe it myself."

It Can Happen So Fast

Veteran's Day was Monday that year. Her Dad had served in Korea. He was part of the VFW and served as part of the honor guard at funerals. Now his comrades would be there for him.

The funeral was on Wednesday of that same week. Noel and Angela drove up on Monday. Glenn arrived on Tuesday. It was a tenuous time to say the least.

When Angela saw her brother for the first time in years, she didn't recognize him at first. He had changed in many ways. He used to have straggly hair and a beard to match. He used to always be all slumped over and gave the impression he was a 90-pound weakling.

He drove up and got out of his car. Military haircut and a buff physique was what she saw. He stood straight and tall. He had eyes that could see right through you. He didn't presume anything as he approached Angela. Instead he was very cautious. He knew the hurt he had put her through.

He first went to his Mom and gave her a big hug. Releasing her he looked her in the eye with tears of his own. "I am so sorry Mom."

"I know. I know."

And then he looked at Angela. He licked his lips and then said, "Can I give you a hug Angela?"

She didn't know what drove her to do it but before he could advance any closer, she wrapped her arms around him and started crying. "Of course you can. Of course, you are my brother."

And then he said, "I know we need to talk. Or, rather, I need to talk... about so many things."

"WE need to talk. But not now. Not today. Today we grieve. Okay?"

"Okay."

They both were crying.

The Plummers

Thanksgiving was approaching. It was a day to be thankful for the many wonderful blessings God had given. It was a day for family to come together no matter how disjointed it had been at times over the year. Time to put things in the past and leave them there.

Well, they were all going through the motions, but this Thanksgiving would be like no other ever in their household. After that fateful day in the office of the Examiner when George said what he said and Arlene said what she said, things just were not the same. And how could they be?

After George said what he did, he knew he should have kept his mouth shut. But he didn't. He can see himself saying it like in an out of body existence. "You aren't in trouble are you?"

He could try and defend himself by thinking that he wasn't assuming Arlene was pregnant. But that would be a lie. Why did he say that? Why? He asked himself that question a million times and never got an answer.

And that same night he was going to apologize. He was going to have a heart to heart with Arlene and beg her forgiveness. That was the plan. But Arlene didn't come home till late. She had been out with friends, he assumed. Brian for sure and probably Brenda and Jared. And he was sure they didn't have anything good to say about him. And he deserved it. And then some.

He heard her come in. It was late. They were in bed. He heard the front door slam. And then he heard her bedroom door slam even harder. No talk would take place tonight. Maybe tomorrow night.

Tomorrow night was the same and maybe even worse. Delaying their talking with one another only made things worse if that was possible.

And then the week passed. George and Vera ate supper alone. No smiles. No conversation. Some Thanksgiving this year, huh.

Eventide '96

"Oh Christmas Tree, Oh Christmas Tree." They could hear the crowd joining in after the first phrase was sung by a soloist this year. The only lights lit were on the Christmas tree. Everyone was at a feverish pitch awaiting the beginning of the Christmas festival of 1996.

The employees at Hakeman's were not outside adding their voices to the Emerald choir. They were inside moving panels around in the dark to open a whole new showcase for those who would crowd in to see what was on display.

This group included Noel and Angela, Angela's Mom, Joanie, Shirley, and Arlene plus a couple of high schoolers who had worked at Hakeman's at various times during the summer.

"Can you give one more shove? This panel is sticking." Noel was having his first experience with the panels that were supposed to be easily moved into their storage place in the wall.

Arlene said, "Can you help me Shirley? It is sticking just like it did last year." Between the two of them, everything fell into place. And not too soon as lights were coming on outside in great array.

"Hit the switch, Ange," Noel yelled out and right in conjunction with every other store the lights of Hakeman's were encouraging, welcoming the crowd. And just like last year, it seemed Hakeman's got the larger part of those shopping that night.

But other stores were also seeing an uptake. The new ice cream shop, that was how it was referred to rather than the fancy name, was offering their version of hot cider which went over pretty well. And the new electronics store had holiday CDs on sale.

Brian found himself equally busy at Richards Clothing. Christmas ties, whether silly or elegant were a big draw in the Men's department. In the Women's department festive dresses and blouses announced the season. And then, of course, Christmas sweaters took center stage. Some would sell out quickly. Others, not so much.

It was a busy night up until around 8:30. Shopping slowed down after that. You can only take so much excitement. And this was just the beginning of Eventide. Slowly the downtown parking area gave up the vehicles that took the best spaces they could.

How Was Your Thanksgiving?

Brian got off earlier than Arlene and was on his way over to Hakeman's. They hadn't been together since Wednesday night and Brian was curious how Thanksgiving went over at the Plummers.

"Busy night?" Brian asked as he helped Arlene with her coat.

She looked up at him, smiled and responded, "Oh, yeah. But not near as much fun as last year."

"Why's that?"

"Well, I didn't have you to keep me company."

"Yeah, that was fun." Then Brian asked the big question, "How was your Thanksgiving?"

The tension in the Plummer house had been easing up since the big blowout between Arlene and her father. But there was still that undercurrent that revealed something was not quite right.

So, for the first time in a while they invited George's brother, Art, and his wife to join in the festivities. They came down from Mallard. Art was retired.

"Well, we had Uncle Art and Aunt Mildred for Thanksgiving. We ate around two or so. I think mom and dad thought having them over might make it more ... joyful."

"Did it?"

"I don't know. After the meal I spent most of the time in my room, bored to death."

"You should have called me."

"I thought about that a lot. But ... I don't know. It wasn't a good day. Then again, we haven't had a good day at home for a long time. I was really looking forward to being at the store all day and being with you tonight."

Budget Time

Ever since the scrap with her father, things were a little different between her and Brian, too. It really put a damper on everything. There was still passion between them but not as much as before. Then again, maybe time had something to do with it. Still they were committed to being together.

"Did you take a look at that budget Rachael gave you?" Brian thought a change of topic might be a good idea.

"Yeah, I did." Arlene got excited about this new topic. "I liked it. I think we could manage it."

Brian smiled, "I think so too. Even if we didn't get a raise in pay for a while, our combined income would pretty much take care of everything."

"Well, not everything. I mean, we might have to still watch what we spend and maybe not eat out so much."

"But Arlene, we will have our own home and it will be cheaper eating at home and Jared and Brenda can come over anytime." Brian was getting excited. "Don't you think?"

"Oh, I agree." Then she added, "Have you thought about furniture?"

"Yes I have. We wouldn't have to get all new furniture. We could get some used."

Arlene scrunched up her face, "You want to sit on a sofa with someone else's germs on it?"

"Well, I never thought about that."

And they went on to discuss what else they needed to buy. And this put them in a very good mood, thinking of their own place. And then they got off topic talking about kids and what the future might hold in store.

And that led to romance and a drive around the lake.

The Dahlke's

"Bet you didn't think I would be around to help you again this year, did you?"

"No Mom, I definitely didn't. But I am glad you were here... are here. I would never have guessed all the changes that would be taking place this year." Angela sat down with a glass of eggnog.

Noel put his hand over hers. "We weren't even engaged last year at this time."

Joanie added, "And Marvin was still around." They were all thinking about the past. "It will be sad without him at Christmas."

"Yeah," Angela agreed. "It was sad not having him here for Thanksgiving." Everyone got a little melancholy.

After enough time had passed, Noel tried to lift up spirits by asking, "Joanie, do you have any idea whether you will move or not? I mean, you were talking about coming back to Emerald. Anymore thoughts?"

"Well, I don't want to rush into anything, but I have been thinking." She hesitated a little bit before going on. "Young America and the lake was all your Dad's idea. And I didn't mind, but I don't like the idea of being on that lake all by myself through the winter."

Angela said, "I don't blame you. You know, I heard they were thinking about building apartments for seniors here in Emerald."

"Really?"

"Don't remember who told me, but how does that sound?"

"Well, depending on how big one might be, that doesn't sound bad."

Noel said, "I will look into that and see where plans are at. Maybe I can help move things along."

Dinner Conversation

Six people were enjoying a Sunday meal in the Emerald household on this the first Sunday in Advent. Jeff and Anita, Jake and Rachael and Jared and Emily.

"The church looked beautiful today,' Emily said. "How do they get all those decorations up so fast after Thanksgiving?"

"It takes a lot of teamwork," Jeff said and then took a bite of meatloaf. He hadn't helped with it this year, but he had in the past.

Jake smiled as he grabbed a dinner roll and put an ungodly amount of butter on it. "I tell you; I wouldn't be on that ladder putting up that garland all the way to the top."

"Me either," His dad agreed. "But for the church to look so nice, someone has to do it."

"A lot of people in church today," Rachael added.

"Yeah and it will be that way until Christmas."

"Got a question," Anita said looking at Jared. "I saw Brian sitting with Arlene in church, but they weren't with Arlene's parents. I was wondering why?"

"They were sitting in church together? Brian doesn't go to our church."

Jared said, "Yeah, but Arlene does, and they are getting pretty serious."

"Really?" Anita asked. "I didn't know that. How serious?"

"Well, he gave her a Promise Ring a while back and I wouldn't be surprised if she gets an engagement ring for Christmas."

Rachael looked over at Jake who wasn't following the conversation at all and teased him, "What do you think about that?"

"About what?"

"Arlene and Brian getting engaged."

He just shrugged his shoulders. So much for teasing him about his old girlfriend.

"But why weren't they sitting with Arlene's parents?" Anita was puzzled.

Jared knew the answer but was not going to tell anyone yet.

The Dreaded Knock

It wasn't just the knock but the words coming after it.

"Arlene, can we come in and talk to you for a minute?"

She opened the door and said, "Why don't we do any talking we have to do in the living room."

"Wherever you feel comfortable, dear," her mother said.

Arlene sat in the chair and her parents sat on the couch.

Nobody said anything for a few seconds. Arlene broke the silence. "What do we have to talk about?"

Her mother looked at her. Her dad was looking down at first but then spoke. "Arlene, I want to apologize to you about what I said a few weeks ago when you came to my office."

Arlene just sat there.

"I would have apologized later that day, but you didn't get back home until we were in bed. And I got the feeling you didn't really want to talk to me then anyway. And... well... I am sorry it took me so long to say this."

Arlene didn't smile or show any emotion.

"Arlene, I love you..."

And her mother added, "We both love you."

Her dad took over again. "And it is killing us with what is happening to our family. We are so sorry about all of this."

Arlene looked down. A tear was starting to form in her eye. She caught it with a tissue. She hated to see how hurt her parents were.

She sat there and finally looked up at her dad. "Dad, you really hurt me that day, asking me if I was in trouble."

"I know. I know."

"Let me finish. I have always looked up to both of you and tried to do all the things you wanted me to do. And I want you to know that I love both of you as well. These past few weeks have not been easy for me either." She looked down, not sure how to continue.

Her parents let her take her time.

"But you should know that I love Brian as well. And it is not some silly crush. We are serious about getting married someday. And we are saving our money and trying to figure out if we can afford to do it. I think we are being very responsible. Daddy, you said you were proud of how responsible I was. Well, I am responsible. I get good grades in all my classes. I am learning photography, and my mentor thinks I have a future there if I want it. Angela Hakeman trusted me to take care of her store while she was on her honeymoon." She stopped for a moment and was going to continue on.

“But, Arlene,” her mom had some things to say. “We do think you are responsible, but this relationship with Brian... yes he is nice... but Arlene, don’t you think you are too young? I mean really!”

Arlene started to shake a little. “That is it, huh? If we want to get engaged or ... even get married... is that going to be ... are you going to try to stop us?”

“Arlene...”

“No Dad, what are you saying?”

“Arlene, we are not going to try to stop you. It is just...”

The silence was deafening. Finally, Arlene got up, got her coat, and headed for the door.

“Arlene, where are you going.”

“I don’t know.” And she was gone.

George and Vera

They both sat there as they felt the door slam. They heard the car start and take off rather abruptly.

Vera started to cry, and George pulled her close.

"What is going to happen to our beautiful little girl?"

"She is not so little anymore. And she has a mind of her own."

"What do you think she is going to do? Do you think she and Brian are going to get engaged?"

George took a deep breath. "I don't think there is a thing we can do to stop it if they do. They are old enough. They don't need our permission."

Vera started to cry even more. And through her tears she said, "What are we going to do?"

Without any expression, he said, "I think we need to support them and help them if they are really serious about getting engaged."

"But they are so young."

"We can say that until we are blue in the face, but it is not going to change a thing. I don't want to build a wall between us and our daughter, now or ever."

Pop's

After talking with Rachael about a budget to find out how much it would cost to rent an apartment Brian and Arlene got very excited. They could see their future living in something like that, starting their life together. And in a way, they wanted to decide this on their own... a lot of things on their own.

But when big decisions had to be made it seemed that Brenda and Jared were always in on it to some degree.

"So, your talk with your parents didn't go so well?" Brenda looks over at Arlene.

"It was a disaster."

"What did they say?"

"Well, Dad did apologize for what he said. And I appreciated that."

"You mean when he thought you were pregnant?"

"Yeah. But after that it all went downhill. Too young. Too young. Too young! That is all I heard." She stopped for a moment. "I just had to get out of there."

"So what now?" Brenda asked. It seemed these two were having a conversation on their own. The guys were just sitting and listening.

"Well," Arlene said. Then she looked at Brian, "What do we do?"

Brian looked around at the other three. They were waiting for him to respond, to say just the right words. Finally, he said, "You know, I think we should just slow down..."

"Slow down? What do you mean, 'Slow down?' Have you changed your mind about us?" Arlene didn't like what she heard.

"Listen." Brian pulled her close and looked into her eyes. "I have not changed my mind. I would marry you right here and now if I could. But what I am thinking is that we, you and I, keep this planning going on and on, like nothing bad has happened. We get engaged, but don't set a wedding date just yet. At least we don't tell anyone. Let everyone get used to the fact that we are engaged. Let it settle in for a while. And after everyone is comfortable with that, then we announce a date. What do you think about that?"

"Well how long will we have to wait? Until we are old and wrinkled? Maybe in our 30s?" Arlene had doubts.

"No, in my mind I am thinking next year sometime." He looked at Arlene. "What do you think?"

She started to get a grin on her face. "I knew there was a reason I fell in love with you. You are so logical. Let's try it."

"Okay. First thing is we have to get engaged. Do you want to go with me to get the ring? Or do you want to be surprised?"

"Surprise me with all of it!"

The Request

He knew she was in school. He saw her take off for Alcoa and knew she would be gone for a long time. All morning, in fact. She didn't know what he had in mind and if she did, she might have vetoed the whole idea. He wanted to do it anyway.

As he walked up the street, it was only a few doors, his resolve became stronger. If he was going to be a man, he had to do this. It was only right.

As he opened the door, he received a smile at first and then it dropped to the floor.

"Mr. Plummer, can I talk to you for a minute."

He paused before responding. "Sure Brian, come in. Have a seat." He motioned him to sit in the same chair Arlene sat in so many weeks ago. "What's on your mind?"

"Well, Mr. Plummer, I know you know about me and Arlene. Arlene has told you about how serious we have gotten about one another. And I know you have, uh, some reservations about our getting married."

George let him continue to talk.

"And I am not here, Arlene doesn't even know I am here, not to get you to change your mind or anything like that. But I am here to ask your permission to ask her to marry me." Sensing George was going to say something Brian held up his hand. "Now, I know you think we are too young, and maybe we are, but this is just an engagement right now. While we plan to get married in the future, right now we just want to make it public and get engaged. Marriage, a wedding would be sometime in the future. I don't know when, but for right now, I am asking you if I have your permission to ask her?" When George didn't say anything, Brian continued, "Well, do I?"

"And if I say NO?"

Brian just sat there. "NO?"

"Yeah, what would you do then?"

Brian rubbed his forehead. "I don't know Mr. Plummer. I wanted to do this right. I wanted to show you respect by asking you before I asked Arlene. Mr. Plummer, Arlene loves you like you wouldn't believe, and it is tearing her up inside, this whole thing. She wants your blessing. I want your blessing."

George said, "The answer is NO!"

Brian looked him in the eye. There was a stare down for a while. Then Brian slowly got up and headed towards the door.

"You are still going to get engaged, aren't you?"

This question surprised Brian. He turned around with one hand on the door, "Yes," he looked down and then back at George, "we probably are."

Silence.

"Then come back and sit down. We need to talk."

Guess What

That afternoon when Arlene was working at Hakeman's, Brian came over on his break.

"Well this is a nice surprise." Arlene teased. "Are you here to pick up something for your girlfriend. And if you don't have one, I am available." She gave a coy smile.

He slid his hand around her waist. And as no one was watching he gave her a quick kiss. "Got some news for you."

"What is it?"

"Oh, no. Not so fast. This is special news. Has to be delivered in a special way."

"What did you have in mind?"

"Let's go out to the lounge at The Dock for appetizers tonight."

"Oooh, sounds good. Pick me up after work? Am I dressed appropriate for such news."

He raised his eyebrows. "Oh, you are dressed just fine."

They ordered some appetizers and were waiting for the order to come.

"Well, what's the news? You've made me wait long enough."

"The news is... I talked to your dad today."

Her expression immediately changed. "Talked about what?"

"I told him I was there to ask permission to marry you."

Arlene wondered why this was brought up. "And what did he say?"

"I laid it all out before him. I told him how much I respected him, and I wanted to get his blessing and so on and so forth."

"Again, what did he say?"

Pause. "He. Said. No."

"Oh, this is a great way to start the evening."

"Now wait. Now wait. When he said that, I got up and went to the door. Didn't say anything to him. Then he asked. You're still going to get engaged aren't you?"

"What did you say?"

"I said yes."

"And then you left?"

"No. He asked me to sit down again, that there was more to talk about."

"And did you?"

"Yes. We talked about a lot of things. And bottom line, we are going to get engaged."

"Right," Arlene said. "Before I am an old maid."

"How about right now?" Brian pulled the ring out of his pocket and said, "Arlene Plummer, would you marry me?"

Arlene was stunned. Didn't expect it at this time or this place, but readily accepted. No one else in the place knew what had just happened. And they would keep it quiet for a week so as to not make it look like right after he had talked to her dad that they got engaged. By the way, Brenda and Jared found out later that night.

May I See Your Ring Please

A week later Brian and Arlene shared the news with her parents, and everything was civil, and it seemed the relationship with her parents was back on track.

Then they went to his parents and announced the news. There was a little more excitement here. No one's little girl was being stolen.

And then, the next day both workplaces got the announcement, and everyone wanted to see her ring. Everyone wanted to know when the big day was. They were told that they hadn't decided as of yet.

Brian and Arlene were together in church every Sunday and now they were sitting with her parents as well.

Eventide '96 progressed through the month of December. And it was another very profitable and emotional success. It wasn't always about the money.

Christmas Eve with the Dahlke's

"Well, I certainly didn't expect to be here on Christmas Eve this year."

"Well, Mom we didn't expect it either. No one did. But here we are ."

Noel added, "And we are glad to have you. You are always welcome here Joanie.

"What about me?" He asked as he tried to look a little sad about why no one was saying good things about him.

Angela poked him in the side and said, "Hey big brother, we have a lot of Christmases to make up for."

Glenn took the opportunity to give her a hug.

Joanie gave a motherly smile. "I am so glad that my children are on good terms with one another again. I only wish your father could be here."

"We do too, Mom, but in a way, if he hadn't died when he did, well... it sounds kind of bad but..."

"You two wouldn't have reconciled like you did." Joanie added.

Glenn thought for a moment. "Well your wedding had something to do with it as well."

"And your letter," Angela added.

"Yes, I thought it was about time I manned up and put an apology down in writing."

The reconciliation between Angela and Glenn brought the family together. Who knows if they will be closer geographically at some future time. No one was about to guess on that.

"Well, are we going to open presents or just look at them?"

"Angela. Angela. You haven't changed a bit. You couldn't ever wait to find out what you got."

"Okay. Okay. I will do what I did so many years ago. I will distribute the gifts." She got off the couch and looked for a special box with Noel's name on it.

"I have to say something first," Glenn was looking at Angela. "Angela, when I saw you at your wedding, I was sincere in saying how pretty you looked. And as I look at you now, you are even prettier." Then looking at Noel he continued, "And you are one lucky guy!"

"Tell me about it!" Noel smiled.

"Enough of that," Angela said. "Well, maybe not." She grinned.

"Okay, Noel, you get the first gift."

"Hmm. What could this be? He shook the box. I guess a pen and pencil set." He unwrapped the box, opened it and had a look on his face that showed he didn't know what it was. He picked it up. "What in the world? What is this Ange?"

With her nose in the air, she said, "Haven't you ever seen a positive pregnancy test before?"

Christmas Eve with the Plummers

There was enough of an understanding between George and Brian that the Eventide season was better when it ended than when it started. And Arlene's parents accepted the fact that their daughter had an engagement ring on her finger. The understanding as far as George and Vera were concerned was that wedding plans would be a while in the future.

At any rate, Christmas Eve was a joyous time at the Plummer household. They were all getting ready for the Christmas Eve service at St. Paul's. Getting there early was a must, if you wanted to get a good seat... any seat really.

Brian and Arleen sat by themselves at the beginning of December but that had all changed the rest of the month. They joined Arlene's parents and that was a good thing. There were enough rumors going around the way it was. "What is going on with that Arlene Plummer and the Seagren boy?"

But tonight there was going to be a change for a couple of families. The Emerald family usually took up pretty much one pew as they all sat together. But for this special service and special time in their lives, Jared and Brenda sat with Brian and Arlene. Well, some thought, things are always changing.

The two couples spent some time talking after the service concluded. But it was so crowded that they didn't get much visiting in. No matter, they would be together tomorrow night to compare notes.

The plan for Brian and Arlene was to open presents at her place and then drive to his parents' house and open presents there. In their minds, this was the last Christmas that they would each be single.

Not everybody had that same idea.

Pop's

"Well, you two look like you have a lot on your mind." Brenda could read Arlene like a book. "Something happen?"

Brenda and Jared slid into the booth across from Brian and Arlene.

"Yeah, something happened."

"Oh boy," Brenda asked, "What now?"

Arlene looked at Brian and Brian said, "Go ahead and tell them."

"Well," and she took a deep beath, "we found out last night that my parents are okay with us being engaged but definitely NOT getting married for a couple years."

"What?" Brenda said, "A couple of years! Why?"

"The same old reason, too young."

Brenda just shook her head.

"And then we went over to Brian's place thinking things would be different. You know Brian's dad supports us, but he doesn't say much. Well, his Mom had a lot to say. I think she talks to my Mom a lot. Bottom line, they feel the same."

"What are you going to do?"

Arlene looked at Brian and then a side glance at Jared and Brenda. "We have some thoughts."

New Year's Day

New Year's Eve at the Kemps had become an institution, so to speak in Emerald. This was a party like no other. While it started years ago with just the Kemp family and the Emerald family getting together, as you might expect. Now, tons of people thought they were invited as well.

It was basically an adult crowd by this time. Jared and Brenda along with Brian and Arlene were present as were their parents although they weren't all together.

The kids had plans just like they did last year. And after making an appearance at the party the two couples took off. Not much was thought about it. Neither family showed any concern.

People usually sleep in on New Year's Day. And that is normally because they don't go to bed too early. It was about ten the next morning that most people were up and ready to watch the Rose Parade in Pasadena.

Vera knocked and then slightly opened Arlene's door like she did quite often. The room was empty. The bed was made. Where was she?

They called Brian's place to see if she was over there. "No she isn't here, and neither is Brian. We thought they might be with you."

Only one other place to call and that was the Coopers. "Brenda, are Brian and Arlene with you?"

"Uh, no they're not. Why?"

"We can't seem to find them. You wouldn't happen to know where they are, would you?"

Brenda didn't answer right away. Then she said, "Well, uh..."

Made in the USA
Columbia, SC
15 September 2024

41800416R00163